Blue Wells

Sheriff Rufus Stone has good cause for keeping a vigilant eye on the town's comings and goings, meting out brutal, uncompromising treatment to drunks and drifters. So when Will Jarrow happens upon Blue Wells, Stone nails him as the usual, itinerant cowboy. But the young stranger is a lot more than that and his provoking behaviour is soon a burr under the wary sheriff's saddle. For two years, Will has lived with dark thoughts about the fateful night that changed his life and grappled with his need for retribution.

How much longer can Will Jarrow pretend to be something he's not? And how much longer will it be before Rufus Stone realizes who he really is?

Blue Wells

Abe Dancer

A Black Horse Western

ROBERT HALE · LONDON

ISBN 978-0-7198-0916-3

Robert Hale Limited
Clerkenwell House
Clerkenwell Green
London EC1R 0HT

www.halebooks.com

Typeset by
Derek Doyle & Associates, Shaw Heath
Printed and bound in Great Britain by
CPI Antony Rowe, Chippenham and Eastbourne

1

'Are you going out there to kill him, Rufus?'

'Not unless I have to. It's up to him.'

'So, don't take your guns.'

'There's hardly anywhere I don't take at least one little smoke pole, Grace. "Out there's" one of 'em.'

'Yes, I know that, Rufus. But right now that young feller's drunk and confused, and probably mean-headed. In an hour or so, you could send Eben out for him. It would be no more difficult than taking down a bum calf.'

The sheriff of Blue Wells showed no sign of weakening in his resolve. He never did. Some called this big man of the law with the fearsome reputation 'Rufus Heart of Stone'. To others he was known as 'Sheriff Stone Dead', because that was the way he brought in most troublemakers and wanted men.

'Calves don't go around robbing banks. Besides, it'll look like the law's gone soft,' Stone replied, while levering a shell into the breech of his Spencer carbine. He shook his head emphatically. 'Can't have that, Grace. County don't pay me to wet-nurse.'

Grace Chard slumped her shoulders and sighed. For the good-looking proprietor of the Chuckwalla Saloon, the outlook had a painful familiarity about it. Grace was one of the few people in town who'd ever attempt to influence Rufus Stone in his duty. But it was a thankless task. The sheriff hadn't collected his pen names for nothing.

'Please, Rufus. His name's Cory Newton, and he's made a mistake . . . a big one. But give him another chance,' she persisted.

Stone drew a crumpled Wanted dodger from an inside pocket of his sack coat. He unfolded it, reading diligently as a few inquisitive onlookers gathered.

'Armed robbery of the Lakewood stage, August 21. Attempted hold-up of Mercantile, Greenfield, November 6. Shooting with intent to kill Assay Agent, Picacho, December 9.' The sheriff lifted his dark, piercing eyes. 'This feller Newton weren't

6

out to give anyone another chance, Grace. And this ain't a page from a dime novel. You want me to read more?' he asked.

'No. What's the point? But he *didn't* kill. And they're only *attempts* because he's not bad blood. There's a difference.' Grace Chard could be just as stubborn, but she lacked the sheriff's clout.

The reason Rufus Stone was able to rule Hondo Basin virtually single-handed was his grit and iron will. He also had a capability with rifle or pistol that gave him the edge over most others. To the town's civic officials, he was the complete lawman – his work unequivocal, simplified by the printed words of a contract.

'You go and explain that difference to the innocent folk he's tried to rob and terrorize,' Stone said. 'You think I should sit and wait till he shoots someone dead? Because he surely will, sooner or later, Grace.' Then he put on his big white hat and went out into the street.

Earlier, Grace had served the young stranger whiskey and a meal. He'd looked rough and wild then, but had treated her with a courteous respect. He smelled of the owl hoot, and Grace had a keen nose for that. She tried to persuade him to leave before getting into more trouble, but he said he was through with running. He wanted a hot meal, a quiet drink and the pleasure of a woman's company. 'I want some hot fixin's an' I'll take me a meal in that,' he'd said, with a callow grin. Grace knew that on the face of it, it was harmless enough behaviour, but potentially tragic in the town where Rufus Stone wore the badge.

After one too many rye whiskies, the keyed-up young braggart had refused Grace's advice to ride on, even to quieten down.

'I'll leave here when I'm good an' ready an' not before,' he'd loudly declared.

And now he was out on the street with an old Dragoon's Colt in his hand, his restless features set into the early-evening breeze. But even drunk, Cory Newton had a keen sense for danger. He stopped abusing a worried storekeeper and put on a wolfy grin, as his dark eyes searched back along the street.

In the saloon, Grace Chard didn't move away from the bar, but everybody else was watching from the front windows when Rufus Stone stepped down from the saloon's overhang.

'Newton, put that gun down.' Stone's voice rang hard and clear down the rapidly emptying street.

Looking as though he was proud to be challenged, Newton lifted his chin. He struck a pose, holding the Colt away from his side. 'You talkin' to me, badgepacker?' he challenged.

But Stone didn't back off. He didn't know how. Instead, he took a step forward and raised the barrel of the carbine.

Cory Newton was too full of booze and bravado to be much impressed or scared. For a few long seconds, he watched Stone get closer before he made a move. *This beats the hell out of arguin' with my horse,* he thought. He used his thumb to set the action, swinging up the big Colt towards the oncoming sheriff.

'I told you to put the gun down, kid,' Stone called out. 'I can't have you shooting me or anyone else.'

Don't get more excitin' than takin' out a goddamn lawman, was Newton's flawed thought as he pulled the trigger of his Colt. He didn't have time to rue the mistake, only staying alive long enough to feel the first of Stone's bullets hammering into his chest.

Grace Chard hugged herself at the sudden eruption of gunfire, shivering, as through cold. The more quixotically minded in Blue Wells thought the saloon keeper was carrying a torch for Rufus Stone. That she could harbour a deeper feeling was beyond their wit.

Whatever Grace Chard felt for the sheriff, she

wasn't going to observe the gunfight in the street, though. She knew there would be someone sprawled dead and bloody in the hard-packed dirt, stood over by someone who looked as if they'd no choice but to kill. It was as inevitable as daybreak that any lawbreaker who'd dare to cross Stone's path would end up roped to a plank, photographed with their own Wanted notice tucked into their pants.

The prints which ornamented Stone's office were reasons why Grace never visited. The sheriff claimed the pictures acted as a deterrent to the lawless, but Grace believed there was more to it than that. She held they fed a sickness inside Rufus Stone, something that she hoped someday to cure. But it wasn't going to be there and then, she thought, pouring herself a badly needed whiskey.

Less than thirty yards away, the sheriff stood under the gaze of an admiring throng. He was calling for volunteers to heft the bullet-riddled corpse of hapless Cory Newton down to the photographer's shop. He looked on coldly as a group of men carted the body away, betraying no emotion at the bloody work he'd done. But his mind posed the same question he asked of himself each and every time someone fell to his gun. *Was that him? He weren't much more'n a goddamn weaner.*

10

At the town's livery, Sourdough Weems eyed the new arrival with interest. 'You some sort o' stock trader?' he asked.

Will Jarrow shrugged. In and around Hondo Basin, most folk were instinctively careful about making such an enquiry.

'Not beef, more the look of a horse wrangler,' the liveryman continued, undeterred.

Will was tall and well made, his hazel eyes as clear as an autumn morning. He gave a tight smile, almost shook his head as he hauled his saddle off his buckskin and onto a saddle tree.

'Don't tell me. You're a lawman, hot on the trail of a wrong'un you've chased clear across the Llano.' But Weems was forced to interrupt his interrogation as a wave of pain gripped his jaw and sent him to the medicine chest.

The liveryman had a cabinet, jam-packed with everything. Bottles labelled and some not, including Prickly Ash Bitters, Oil of Cloves and Quinine Sulphate. Half his weekly earnings went on remedies, but most of them were quack and ineffective. He spent a lot of the time doped to the gills, and right now, his life wasn't filled with light and laughter.

11

Will shook his head good-naturedly as he removed the horse's bridle. 'Water, rub down and feed,' he said, when Weems came back.

The liveryman rolled his eyes, grimacing from a massive belt of Dr Shelly's Juniper Juice. 'Yessir, as I thought first thing. I'll wager you're some sort o' horse peddler,' he persisted stubbornly.

'Then you'd lose,' Will advised.

'Bounty hunter, then? Gambler? Gunslinger? Who or what the hell *are* you, mister?'

Will wasn't always this tolerant. But things were different now, and he'd been a long time in the learning of it. 'Traveller. I'm a traveller, travelling in fumadiddles an' ladies' step-ins,' he answered, half-smiling at his own joke. 'Can't you tell by the look of me?'

Now it was Weems's turn to shake his head and drag out a smile. He didn't know who or what Will Jarrow represented, only that it wasn't any sort of undergarment business. An uneasy thought hit him. 'Well, seein' that hogleg you got tied to your leg, mister. If you're one o' them curly wolfers, you'll—'

'You got any twine?' Will cut in, finally getting riled. 'An' a stitching tool?'

'Stitchin' tool?' Weems frowned. 'What you want one o' them for?'

12

'To sew your goddamn mouth shut next time it opens,' Will retorted as he turned away.

'No need to get so cankered, young feller.' Weems's voice was rising a little as he followed Will to the doorway. 'I was goin' to tell you to watch your tread. If our sheriff sees you so much as spit on the sidewalk, he'll slap some iron on you.'

'Much obliged, but I know about your sheriff,' Will said as he walked on.

Weems leaned in his doorway. 'Only tryin' to help,' he muttered aloud. 'Stop you gettin' into any trouble.' The stranger had intrigued and impressed him, and he pondered wryly on what the outcome would have been if he'd asked his name.

Weems's interest in something that shouldn't concern him was one way of taking his mind off the devilish things going on in his mouth. There were times when the pain was so bad, he even felt a pang of envy for all the road agents and cattle thieves who'd been planked since Rufus Stone was sworn in. *At least their goddamn cutters won't be achin' as much as mine,* he thought, then wondered what it was that the stranger knew about Blue Wells's sheriff.

13

2

It was quiet when Will stepped through the door of the sheriff's office. There was no sound or movement, nothing from the cells, not even a simmering coffee pot atop the stove.

'Hello,' he called, halting by the broad, well-ordered desk. 'Is anybody home?'

The answer was a sound that sent a chill slithering down his back. It was the deliberate, well-oiled click of a gun hammer being pulled back.

He turned steadily to see the sheriff standing in the alcove that lead from the cells. The Spencer carbine that the man held across his body was trained squarely on his forehead. Although he'd never seen Rufus Stone before, he recognized him instantly. One thing *Sheriff Stone Dead* wasn't short of in the territory was publicity.

14

'Hell, you usually welcome all your visitors like this?' he said, after taking a deep breath.

'No, not usually. But you got to bear in mind the times we live in. That this is the sheriff's office, not a goddamn grocery store.' Stone's voice was low and even. 'So state your name an' business, mister.'

'William Jarrow. An' right now I'm a peaceable citizen, not a goddamn homicidal maniac.'

'Yeah, says you. You got any proof o' that?'

Will stared into Stone's penetrating eyes, carefully reached into his breast pocket to produce his billfold. He held it out.

Stone came forward and took it. For a brief moment, the muzzle of the carbine actually pressed against Will's chest. He moved back a pace and flipped through the billfold. It contained a letter and a document that bore the signature of William Jarrow. The sheriff indicated his writing equipment with a nod. 'Do it for me. Make your mark, or whatever.'

Will took up the pen, dipped it in the inkhorn and signed his name.

Stone carefully compared the signatures, took a few long few seconds before passing the billfold back. He held the carbine on Will a moment longer, then eased off the hammer and leaned it against his desk. 'What's your business, Mr Jarrow?'

15

he demanded, without apology or explanation.

'I don't have any. But if I did, it would probably be to mind it. I'm on vacation.'

'Huh. You're takin' a vacation, here in Blue Wells?'

'That's right, Sheriff,' Will replied curtly. 'So perhaps you'd like to explain why you're throwing down on me.'

Stone tapped his star-and-crescent badge. 'This is all the explanation I need, Mr Jarrow.'

'Not in my book it's not. I'd say you were hoping for some sort of shock retaliation . . . hoping for a fight.'

Will's response brought a sharper, keener look to the sheriff's face. 'Huh, so now who's doing the proddin'? It's plain you don't know much about me,' Stone said, after a silent, closer study of Will. 'Else you'd choose your words a lot more carefully.'

Will was now more conscious of the man's disposition. His way and his tone became colder. 'Are you threatening me, Sheriff? I thought we all lived in a society that allowed us to talk back. The law's meant to uphold and protect that right, if it don't much else.'

Stone went very rigid. 'Be careful, Mr Jarrow. Be very careful. There's a lot o' folk in this town who reckon I draw pay to kick the temper out o' those who don't properly respect this office.'

'I'll respect the man, not the hammered-out piece o' tin he hides behind,' Will retaliated.

'God, you are a piece o' work, feller. Maybe I've got to find out if you're brave or just stupid. So, are you goin' to tell me what it is you really want . . . what brought you here?'

'Right now, I want to know who you mistook me for when I came through that door. If it ever happens again, I might not be so accommodating.'

Stone ground his teeth. For a moment, it seemed he might lose control. The man's position of power in the valley was unconditional, virtually absolute. Most people had fallen out of the habit of treating him like a regular citizen. Perhaps without being aware of it, Stone had come to accept that as normal. The only ones who took serious issue with him these days were itinerant outlaws who didn't know better. The gruesome collection of photographs that ornamented his office walls were evidence of that.

Thoughtfully, Stone went to his chair and sat down. He sniffed, tugged on his string tie, adjusted the butt of a belly gun that thrust from behind his belt buckle. Then he put his hands on the blotter and leaned his fingers together to form a tent.

'The reason I got the drop on you's because three days ago, an' not many yards from where I'm sitting, I shot a dose of bad medicine named Cory Newton. Before him there were others . . . quite a few others,' Stone added quietly. His gesture embraced the gallery of dead rogues. 'Most every one o' them's got friends or kinfolk who harbour the notion of revenge. Fact, there's one, maybe two of 'em up there because of it. Am I making myself clear, William Jarrow?'

'Clear enough, Sheriff,' Will nodded in concession. 'It might ease your disposition to learn that I'm not related to any of these men. And to the best of my knowledge, I never knew or heard of 'em either.'

'Yeah, well to take advantage you would say that, wouldn't you?'

Will shrugged and moved for the door. 'It's the truth. So, unless you aim to put a bullet between my shoulder blades, I'll be taking my leave.' With that, Will stepped outside.

In the street, life was moving at ease through the town, its citizens safe and secure while Rufus Stone was in charge.

'You still ain't told me what you're doin' in Blue Wells . . . in my goddamn office,' Stone called out, rising to his feet. 'I'm going to take a quick dislike to you, feller. It could save me a lot o' time.'

'I'm a God-fearing, peaceable man, Sheriff.' An ironic smile ghosted across Will's tanned face. He still regarded himself as most of that, despite all he'd been through, the 500 miles that brought him to Hondo Basin.

'I'll still be watching you,' Stone warned. 'You won't draw breath without my knowing it.'

'I'm not going into hiding, Sheriff.' Will turned for a parting shot. 'I might even come back.'

Stone stood very still, listening to the stranger's steps recede along the boardwalk. He sniffed again, ran the tip of his tongue along his top lip. *I know you're trouble,* he thought. *Can almost taste it.*

Back inside his office, the sheriff unlocked a cabinet drawer and drew out a thick, buckram-bound file. It was one of the most comprehensive accounts of lawbreakers to be found between the Brazos and the Rio Grande. The names, descriptions and records of the most feared lawbreakers, Stone carried in his head. Details of lesser felons were contained within the ordered file.

The records were Stone's preferred reading. Often, he would sit late at night turning pages ornamented with the photographic prints, woodcuts or drawings of the territory's most wanted. Best he could, he kept the file up to date, and

19

although he knew most of the faces by heart, there just may be the one he failed to recognize. *Not even a goddamn mention,* he thought, when after an hour he failed to find any reference to William Jarrow.

3

It was just gone noon the next day when Will walked into the reading corner of Ma Kettle's Mercantile. He wore a blue flannel shirt, denim pants and rawhide weskit. He was a healthy-looking individual, striking, to the patrons of the would-be Blue Wells Library.

'Looks to me like one o' them manhunters,' Will heard an old lady mutter to her companion, as he stepped up to the counter. He smiled wryly, thought of the liveryman and Sheriff Stone, one or two others who had shown much interest in his arrival in town. At least he now knew what a man-hunter looked like, although he was not sure whether it was a good or a bad thing in Blue Wells. The town was a very searching community, with a reputation as a mortal deadfall for outlaws and their like.

But as long as the curiosity wasn't up close and personal, it didn't bother Will. He had taken too many twists and turns, crossed too many rivers for there to be any risk of somebody stumbling on to why he'd travelled full across two states.

Will leaned against the counter, pushed up the brim of his hat and cast an eye along the shelves. Books were an interest and enthusiasm. But it hadn't always been so. His pa never acknowledged reading as necessary ammunition for a growing boy. Ironically, it was a habit Will had acquired in a rock-and-iron-bound place where time hung heavily on every man's hands.

'Good day. May I help you?'

Will turned to meet the direct stare of the severe-looking lady who was walking towards him. She was around his age, her dark hair drawn back tightly in a bun at the nape of her neck.

'Good day,' he returned, removing his Stetson. 'I'm new in town. My name's Jarrow.'

'Yes, I know who you are.'

'It's not often that strangers have that advantage on me,' he said, after a moment's thought.

'I'm sure,' the lady replied, almost smiling back. 'Although this is my Reading Corner. It's a reserve for those with an interest in print. In these parts, a lot of folk prefer to get their stories and news by word of mouth. Perhaps gossip's a better word. Chinese whispers, more accurate.'

Will smiled back. 'I'll wager no one's got to hear of me through the pages of any Daily Trumpet.'

'Well, I don't know about that. I'd heard about the new man in town and his exchange with the sheriff before I'd left here last evening. That went with a full description, of course.'

'Yeah, of course.' Will wondered if the lady's response was a symptom of nervousness. 'That would be in case I came here to run riot among the candy jars and shoot up the dime novels, I suppose. Most of the folk I've met so far seem to think I'm some sort of wild owl hoot.'

'That's nothing to joke about in Blue Wells, Mr Jarrow,' she reproved, going behind the counter.

'Yeah, having met your law officer, I've picked up on that too.'

Will realized that beneath the stern-looking exterior, there was something more agreeable, more attractive. But that was as far as his interest was going. That was buried outside of a town called Santa Rosa.

'You'd be well advised not to annoy the sheriff as you did yesterday, Mr Jarrow.'

'That's a welcome piece of advice. But how do you know how he felt? It was only the two of us at

the jailhouse. Was it him who came in here yesterday evening?'

She shook her head. 'It was his deputy,' she
said. 'Rufus Stone's no gossip.'

'No, just those he confides in,' Will returned
acidly. 'He's the shoot 'em first type.'

That unsettled her. 'What can I do for you?' she
asked briskly.

'You could even up the advantage by telling me
your name . . . your full name.'

'Miss Winney.'

'That's a title, not your full name.'

'April. Now, what was it you wanted? I do have
other work, other customers.'

'There's a copy of *Robinson Crusoe* on the shelf. I
hear it's a good story.'

'It's certainly that,' the lady agreed. 'And most
of the schooled world seems to think so, too.'

Eying April Winney circumspectly, Will paid for
the book. Then he nodded politely and muttered
he was obliged. Feeling the eyes of everybody on
his broad back, he left the store.

The whispering started even before the door
closed behind him. He stopped and glanced back
through the window, catching April Winney
peering out at him. He smiled, mouthed the word
'Boo' and touched two fingers to the brim of his

hat. But the moment of good humour faded as he walked away. Pretending to be interested was all a sham, he knew. Maybe if he could take a genuine interest in another woman the pain would ease. *One thing about this kind of feeling, it adds a little vigour,* he thought wryly as he crossed the street.

The Chuckwalla was already busy with its regular customers. They were mostly workmen from in and around the town. They came to celebrate making it through the morning, deaden the dreariness of a long afternoon.

The handsome woman who had served him the previous night acknowledged him with a nod and a cool smile. He had learned that she was a close friend of the sheriff, thought maybe some of the lawman's hostility had rubbed off on her.

With the storekeepers, clerks and inevitable barflies, most others in the saloon looked dull and complacent. He guessed they probably voted regularly for Rufus Stone. Will learned that not so long ago, there had been a move to have the man installed as both mayor and town sheriff – twin offices that would have succeeded if Stone himself hadn't vetoed it.

To the citizens of Blue Wells, Sheriff Stone was the man they acclaimed for hauling their town from frontier darkness to culture and affluence. It seemed to bother few of them that his methods seemed more akin to that of a contract killer than upholding laws and town ordinance.

But none of that troubled Will, much. Stone's partiality for gunplay was something he might ultimately turn to his own advantage.

He sat at an end table in the saloon, lunched on cheese, boiled eggs and two cold beers. He read the first few pages of his newly acquired book, had a cynical chuckle when young Robinson Crusoe told of his father imparting serious and excellent counsel.

Everybody who came and went in the next couple of hours gave him a thorough looking-over. Then Rufus Stone came in and fixed him with a gimlet eye as he stood at the bar talking with Grace Chard.

Can't figure me out, can you? Will mused, leaning back in his chair. He knew that Stone was intolerant of strangers who rode in to challenge his domineering rule. Whether anybody ever stopped to consider if the sheriff's bigoted attitude towards lawbreakers might attract more trouble than it prevented, was something Will doubted. *Huh, either way, it's obvious that a lot of you folk are waiting eagerly for me to try and blow Stone's head off,* he thought. *But I've already told him, I'm a peaceable*

26

man, here on vacation. He shook his head, glanced down to his book for a few moments, then turned to gaze out the window at the street. *Yeah, fair enough,* he continued, *you'd have to be some ham-head to believe that.*

The food and beer were revitalizing him, and the aches from weeks in the saddle were beginning to ease from Will's body. He knew he'd soon tire of just lazing around Stone's town, of keeping up the pretence. But for now, that was how he'd have to play it. His plans were a long time in the making, and he wasn't about to jeopardize them.

It was late afternoon when he looked up from his reading to see another newcomer to Blue Wells. He was stocky and dark-skinned, wore shoulder-length black hair, and breasted his way confidently through the swing doors.

Although it wasn't obvious, Will knew the man had probably assessed every customer in the saloon before he was halfway to the bar. He cursed under his breath. *And there's us all thinking I was trouble,* he almost said aloud.

4

'Laguna? Laguna Paris?' the saloon girl giggled. 'What sort of name's that?'

'It's on account of my eyes,' the man said quietly. 'And my pa,' he added, fixing the girl with his bright blue eyes. 'What do they call *you*?'

'Honey.'

The man thought for a second. 'Sweet,' he said with a smile. 'We're not so different. What's your particular poison, Honey?'

'Oh, nothing too strong at this time of the day.'

'Two glasses of your best whiskey,' Laguna ordered, establishing his ability to pick someone who likes a drink.

'I like boys from south of the border. They know things,' Honey confided, then downed most of her measure in a single gulp. 'What brings you to Blue Wells?'

Laguna grinned, his face crinkling with amusement. 'If I get lucky, it'll be to kill someone.'

Honey giggled again, not really thinking that the man might be serious. 'Did they do you some harm . . . this someone?' she asked.

'I haven't rode here for the good of my health,' Laguna said, suddenly feeling a shift of the burden he carried within him. Very soon he'd be cancelling a debt, laying claim to the long-sought respect of his father. 'The evil old goat,' he muttered, peering into the mirror along the back-bar. 'Let's drink to tonight,' he toasted. 'We could both get lucky.'

Honey laughed, but a few nearby drinkers scowled. They were old-time bigots, and the spectacle of one of their own hurdy-gurdy girls enjoying herself with a mixed blood didn't sit well with them.

'He'll be stompin' on his hat soon enough. They get drunk on burro's piss,' a man muttered out of the side of his mouth. But for the others, the instinct for staying alive had already kicked in, and they didn't offer more than an offensive frown.

Laguna and Honey were chatting amiably when Grace Chard came downstairs to oversee the start of evening trade. Her first glance was for Will Jarrow, who was still sitting where he'd been when she went upstairs for her catnap an hour ago. Then she swept a professional eye across the room, was moving towards the bar when she was detained by the town's mayor.

'Don't want to find fault with your business, Grace,' the man began, 'but there's customers here who mind about who they're rubbing shoulders with.' He paused to jerk his chin towards Honey and the man called Laguna Paris.

Grace took a deep breath, and smiled thinly. 'Oh, Honey doesn't mind. She's so obliging she'll drink with anyone,' she replied, her look becoming more steely. Grace Chard was one of the few people in Blue Wells who made no distinction between colour and creed. And it had nothing to do with business either. They were all welcome at the Chuckwalla. *But I'll wager she'd like to make an exception with you,* she wanted to snap back. 'Why don't you go and explain your misgivings to her?' she offered carelessly.

Grace lifted the counter flap and went behind the bar to pour herself a single shot. She swilled the liquor around her mouth as though to cauterize a bad taste, then poured another. She moved along to where one of her girls was flirting with the handsome young man with the bright blue eyes.

'Honey lamb,' she broke in. 'You're attracting attention . . . upsetting some of our customers.'

The girl instantly took a small step away from Laguna. 'Sorry, Miss Grace. I was getting carried away. This is Laguna Paris. He's from Mexico,' she said and smiled openly.

When greetings were exchanged, Laguna nodded artfully. 'I'm pleased to meet you, ma'am. If you're a friend of Sheriff Stone Dead . . . *real* pleased,' he said.

'I don't think we know you well enough for that sort of joke. If it *is* a joke,' Grace retorted huffily.

'Well, I'm sorry all the way to Snake City and back, ma'am,' Laguna apologized. 'I guess I've drunk too much. You know about pepper-guts an' firewater,' he grinned.

To hide her annoyance, Grace was about to move away. But she hesitated. 'It sounds like you know Sheriff Stone. Do you?' she put to him instead.

'Only by reputation, ma'am.'

'Hmm. Then why did you say what you did about me being his friend?'

'I just meant that I'd want be on the friendly, welcoming side of him. Don't you reckon that's wise for a stranger in town?'

'Hmm,' Grace muttered again. 'You don't have

to be a stranger.' Moving away, she was only too aware that her question wasn't answered.

From a nearby table, Sourdough Weems raised his hand in greeting. 'Mistress Chard, I'd like you to bring me whiskies,' he requested. 'Set 'em up in front o' me. One for each goddamn dagger o' pain.'

Listening tolerantly to the liveryman, Grace didn't hear what Laguna was saying to Honey.

'Your sheriff's sure got himself some real followers in this town. Disciple-like.'

'Thanks to Rufus Stone, I could walk the streets at night dressed only in my chemise with no fear of gettin' molested. Ain't that somethin'?' Honey slurred a little, sounded like she wasn't too sure it was what she was meaning to say.

'Yeah, I'll bear it in mind,' Laguna replied casually. Then he turned serious in a way that made the girl uneasy. 'I'm wondering if that feller was wearing more than a pair of long johns. Did you see it, Honey?'

'What feller? See what?'

'The shoot-up in the street, last week.'

'Oh, that. Yeah, I saw, but I can't remember much about who he was.'

But Laguna knew who he was. For a brief time, he'd ridden with him. It was during one of his

breakaway periods when he set out to convince his
father that he really was the ring-tailed roarer he'd
always wanted him to be. Laguna and Cory Newton
had never been partners, but death often had a
way of endowing a relationship with something it
didn't have in life.

'But you saw it?' he continued.

'Sure, everybody did. Most folk in here,
anyways.'

'Was it quick?'

Honey shrugged. 'What's quick?' Then, looking
more closely at him: 'Have you got something
gnawing at your liver, chico?' she asked.

'Yeah, this cheap whiskey,' he laughed quickly.

A sharper and more temperate girl might have
detected the unevenness of Laguna's tone, in his
asking about the street shooting. But all Honey saw
was a swarthy young man who got better looking
and more desirable with every slug she downed.
She curled her fingers around his belt and tugged
him gently towards her. Minutes later, they were
still exchanging warm banter when the sheriff
stepped into the saloon.

Even though they rarely created trouble, every
night Stone made routine checks on the saloons.
Trouble usually took the form of a hellraiser drifting into town to get roostered; like the late Cory

Newton. Citizens of Blue Wells and Hondo Basin who had seen how their sheriff quelled a disturbance no longer had the inclination for that sort of life.

But there were still a few drifters and newcomers who weren't aware of how tough and intolerant Rufus Stone was. The outcomes were more than jawbone or rumour, and they usually found out the hard way.

5

Stone stood just inside the batwings. With his carbine resting easy in the crook of his arm, he gave a thin smile at Sourdough Weems who was insulting a big, hard-looking miner. He knew that when the aches inside Weems's head were real bad, he became pugnacious, fearless. Near the bar, he saw Will Jarrow set his glass aside, and push himself slowly away from his table. Then he looked searchingly around him, at hands and faces among low roils of tobacco smoke. He nodded when Grace smiled, let his attention settle on Honey and her companion.

The young man was new in town and, in Stone's judgement, already moving towards trouble of some kind.

As Stone walked towards the crowded bar,

Honey withdrew her hand from Laguna's waist. She was uncertain about how Stone would feel about her mixing with a half-breed, but certain he'd let on soon enough.

'Good evening, Honey,' the lawman said, tipping his hat, cutting his piercing eyes to Laguna. 'I don't think I know your friend here.'

'This is Laguna, Sheriff,' Honey replied, turning to Laguna, who was leaning crookedly against the bar, grinning. But moments ago he'd been sober as a preacher, if not quite as self-denying. 'What's come over you?' she added in surprise. 'You're lookin' skunk drunk.'

'Evenin' to you, Sheriff,' Laguna slurred, waving unsteadily. 'Fascinatin' town you got here. Closed up tighter'n a gopher's chuff.'

Distaste worked Stone's features, yet at the same time he was relaxed. Drunks rarely gave Blue Wells's sheriff much concern. He usually handled them as easily as a child with a puppy dog. But the ever perceptive Stone didn't think the man calling himself Laguna looked like a regular drunk. He was in too good a shape, healthy looking. And a cowboy on a wild night out didn't normally have a Colts' Navy revolver hanging from his belt.

'You'd better ease up on the juice, feller, or you'll find yourself sobering up in one o' my wretched little cells,' he warned.

'I don't know what's come over him, Sheriff,' Honey defended. 'He was all right a minute ago. It must have hit him quick. You know what they say about these south-o'-the-border fellers. . . .'

'It's the fresh air, Sheriff. Hit me when you come through the door,' Laguna continued, grinning.

'Anything wrong here, Rufus?' Grace edged along the bar after breaking up the wrangle between Sourdough Weems and the miner. She glanced at Laguna, then at Stone for an answer.

The sheriff looked very stern. 'You know I don't like customers being served this much liquor, Grace,' he said.

'He's done this lickety split, and without me knowing. He's not been in here that long. Honey?'

'Yeah. One minute judge, next minute skunk,' Honey chimed in with an expressive, broad smile. 'Goddamn weirdest thing I ever saw.'

'Watch your tongue,' Grace chided.

'Sorry, Miss Grace, I meant *durndest* thing.'

Stone shook his head tolerantly. He studied Laguna, who was now pushing against the bar with an exaggerated sway.

'If these two ladies are right, feller, I'm tryin' to figure out what game you got in mind by playing *borracho*. You got someplace to stay tonight?'

'Don't rightly recall that, Sheriff.'

'Where's your horse? Assuming you didn't crawl here.'

'Tied-in behind the bank. Seemed safest place.'

'You got a bed ground?'

'Tied-in behind the horse behind the bank.'

'Then I suggest you get back there an' sleep it off. I'd do it pronto if I was you, an' stay out of my way.'

'That's wise advice, Señor,' Grace agreed. 'You've done enough drinking this night. Believe me.'

'I'll walk with you,' Honey offered. 'We wouldn't want any harm coming to you.'

'Jus' finish my shot,' Laguna slurred, reaching out for his glass. 'Paid good money.'

Stone looked at Grace. 'If he *has* paid for it, pour it away,' he said tersely.

'Yeah. Sheriff wouldn't want to go shootin' another drunk, would he?' Laguna glared angrily.

Stone appeared to be turning away in disgust. Before he could make a considered response to the slur, there was a sharp warning from near the end of the bar.

'Stone, look to your back.' Will Jarrow had been watching Laguna Paris ever since he'd entered the saloon. Now he was intrigued by the man's sudden slide into mouthy drunkenness. *Whatever he's up to, it's about to happen,* he thought. As he shouted, he saw Laguna's character swiftly change back to sharp concentration. He saw one shoulder flexing, fingers curling as they reached for the Colt.

But Rufus Stone's reaction was lightning fast, almost as if he'd been counting for the 'off'. He made a half turn away from Grace Chard, the muzzle of the carbine bearing unswervingly to Laguna's chest.

The weapon was so close that the powder blast scorched Laguna's shirtfront. His body leapt with a great spasm and hurtled backwards, slamming into a table. As he slid slowly to the floor, his eyes stared sightlessly down at the smoke and spread of blood that oozed from his shirt. The tension left his body and his head rolled to one side. His black hair fanned across the puncheon floor, and he died with the unfired revolver locked rigid in his hand.

Apart from a deep, gulping choke from Honey, the silence in the saloon was instant. Violence had erupted and been resolved so fast that some customers in the Chuckwalla still weren't certain what had happened. But those closer to the bar knew that if it hadn't been for the warning of Will Jarrow, it would have been their sheriff sprawled lifeless at their feet.

'Good God!' Grace exclaimed in shock. 'What happened?'

'He was about to shoot me,' Stone grunted. Then he dropped to one knee and went through the dead man's pockets. He found some dollars, a clasp knife, a handful of betel nuts and a crumpled handwritten letter. In a buttoned pocket tucked behind his belt was a piece of paper folded wadded into a small square.

Stone got to his feet and unfolded what was an old Wanted dodger. It had been issued in Fort Sumner, and was offering a two-hundred-and-fifty dollar reward for information leading to the arrest of suspected road agents, Cory Newton and Laguna Paris.

'There's always a reason, Grace. Always a goddamn reason,' Stone said, looking at the corpse accusingly. 'An' there'll be others,' he murmured, as though thinking aloud. 'Even the scouring of dirt's got to be avenged.'

'It's the sort of vengeance that keeps you in work, though, Sheriff,' Will Jarrow spoke up, and every nearby face swung towards him.

'What's that you say?' Stone demanded as the words sank in.

'Why else did you kill him? You could have smacked him with your gun barrel. He'd have hung, anyway.'

A nerve ticked below Stone's hard eye. 'I'm obliged for your help here, Mr Jarrow,' he grated. 'But that don't include your bootless opinions. For a while there, the Mex had me fooled . . . had us all fooled.'

Will was certain he could have struck the man down had he been in the sheriff's place and he doubted he was as fast as Rufus Stone. 'I suppose we all get the law we deserve,' he declared angrily. Then, with a gesture of disgust, he turned his back and started shouldering his way towards the batwings.

'Jarrow,' Stone snarled out. 'You get your hide back here. You don't walk away from me until I've finished, goddamnit.'

But Will didn't pause, didn't even turn his head. 'You got judge, jury and executioner all rolled into one. Out of my way, fatso,' he swore, shouldering aside a short, portly customer.

Another silence gripped the saloon. Citizens of Blue Wells weren't accustomed to seeing their redoubtable marshal spoken to in the way that Will Jarrow just had.

Rufus Stone knew it too, and wasn't taking it well. 'Who the hell docs he think he is, speakin' to me like that?' he said irately.

'He just saved your life, Rufus. Maybe he thinks that gives him some right,' Grace Chard suggested impassively.

6

Carlo's Jug was a lowly, uncared-for joint, set town-side of the old tannery and the graveyard at the north end of town. It was a false-fronted structure which often looked in danger of folding into the rank watercourse that carried waste from the leatherworks. The interior was gloomy and cheer-less, a place where customers clustered around an open fire and a tough saloon keeper poured some of the most distasteful drinks in the territory.

The Jug didn't only cater for Blue Wells's diverse low life, it was also a haven for any respectable citizen who occasionally wanted to drink alone. Sourdough Weems ran a successful business enter-prise in the main street and took a seat on the town's trade council. Whether he was reputable or not was uncertain. At the Chuckwalla, so-called friends soon tired of his boorish conduct. But Carlo's Jug was a place where he could be as aggressive and obnoxious as he pleased without anybody taking much offence.

It was after midnight when the liveryman weaved unsteadily through the Jug's front door. True to form, he perversely wanted the position at the bar which was occupied by the biggest man around.

'Shift your rump, Lincoln,' he snarled, giving the massively beamed blacksmith a shove. 'Goddamnit, a few more pounds an' you could join a sideshow.'

'One day soon I'm going to take a pair o' bolt tongs an' yank them rotten pegs from your rotten head myself. You see if I don't,' Lincoln retaliated gamely.

But Weems was impervious to such threats. Everything derogatory that could be levelled about the man's pathological aversion to the dentist's chair had been said. Friends of long standing now avoided him because his entire body and most of his clothes were steeped in and stank of the vile potions he sluiced around his jaws. His wife slept elsewhere because she couldn't take his complaints, nightly contortions and bawling any longer. 'No man who endures that sort of toothache twenty four hours a day is going to feel any pain in an insult,' she'd said wearily.

'Hey, barkeep, gimme two fingers o' corn,' he ordered Carlo, who was already reaching for a bottle. Behind the bar was a menu that said you could buy tiger milk, tonsil paint or craw rot. But no matter what you ordered, you got corn whiskey. Some said that Carlo's corn from an unlabelled bottle did a better job of curing hides than most anything they used at the tannery.

Weems slugged his potion down and massaged his lower face. 'I seen some damn funny stuff when I'm roostered,' he said to nobody in particular. 'Now, tonight I just seen the damndest. I saw some feller look out for ol' Rufus, then act like he was about to stiff him himself. Yessir, it was the damndest thing—'

He broke off when Carlo leaned towards him across the bar. The man nodded, indicating somewhere to Weems's right. Weems spilled his drink, cursing as he turned to look.

There was someone standing at the far end of the plank bar. He was nursing a glass in his hand, staring at the bottle in front of him.

'Jeesus, that's him. Will Jarrow. Me an' him go way back. He travels in ladies' unmentionables,' Weems said with a drunken chuckle. 'Hey!' he called out. 'What you doin' in this godforsaken hole, Jarrow? There's folk lookin' all over for you. You're some sort o' hero.'

Will fixed the liveryman with a blank stare. 'Heroes today, bums tomorrow,' he muttered.

Weems squinted back at him. 'Yessir, that's you all right. Never had a lot to say. But I know that if half the town wanted to stand me a drink, I wouldn't be huffin' in this roachtrap. What's grippin' you, son?'

Will dropped his head, stared at the gleaming swill on the bar top. 'It's about best-laid plans,' he replied quietly.

'What the hell are you talkin' about? Make sense, why don't you?'

Will stared at him but didn't seem to see him. 'This place ain't what I had it cut out to be. It's full of busybodies giving the impression they care.'

Weems's face twisted with confusion. 'Are you talkin' about what happened back at the Chuckwalla, son? Has Sheriff Stone got somethin' to do with this?'

Will looked as though he'd noticed Weems for the first time. 'Yeah, something,' he said. 'Like mice an' men.' With that, he stepped away from the bar, turned on his heel and walked straight for the saloon's narrow front door. 'Bet you ain't got that needle an' thread on you,' he added.

Accustomed to being tolerated by people he regularly offended and insulted, Weems was taken aback, almost indignant. 'Well, I'm no goddamn mouse, an' you really ain't no big curly wolfer. Huh, I'm learnin' that,' Weems puffed, looking at the closed faces around him.

'I'd be careful with my mouth if I was you, Soddy,' Carlo said, smirking at his drollness.

'This goddamn horsepiss don't help. I want my money back,' Weems retaliated, as his head began to reel. But his heart wasn't in any verbal combat, because he was trying to hold Will Jarrow in his mind. *What is it between him and the sheriff?* he wondered, frowning thoughtfully as, with a shake of his head, Carlo flooded another whiskey into his glass.

Hardly anyone in Blue Wells used the widespread and usual term of 'boot yard', or 'bone yard', for the town's cemetery. One or two folk on the town council hadn't appreciated the association. Some reckoned that once you were in the ground, the circumstances of your death didn't really matter. So either way it became known as Old Nick's Orchard, or, for the few who remained more conformist, God's Little Acre.

Standing off a way, Rufus Stone drew up the

collar of his coat and puffed out his cheeks. Through the westerly wind, he caught the drift of the preacher's sepulchral voice, heard the bit about returning to the earth, and being lost sheep.

The day was too cold for more than the necessary administrators. Even they had little inclination in ritual ceremony for the outlaw and would-be killer known as Laguna Paris. Honey was there, standing alongside Lenny Loco, the youngster who was minus a few buttons and obsessed with burials of any sort. The undertaker and two bearers, and a couple of workers from the tannery, made up the group of unsympathetic mourners.

Stone didn't remove his hat, and beneath the tugged-down brim, his heavy features betrayed no suggestion of regret or remorse. He attended almost all burials in Blue Wells because he considered it not only his duty, but a fulfilment. That too many men buried in and around the brake of stunt pine had fallen under one of his guns didn't appear to disturb him, and it didn't for most of Hondo Basin, either.

'He came a stranger and died without a friend to hold his hand,' the preacher ended the service.

Stone shook his head in bemusement. *He chose it that way*, was his own conclusion.

The wind suddenly blew colder, swirling

through jimson, over rudimentary markers of wood and stone. Laguna's casket was lowered into the hole and two men dourly shovelled in rock and dirt.

Ten minutes later, Stone rode his grey mare down the stony trail, past the shabby pile of the Jugosa, then up the rise towards the town's main street. For the shortest moment he thought maybe he'd seen the name Paris before and he turned in the saddle. Glancing behind him, he blinked against the wind that lashed his face, the recollection nicking him again when he saw someone standing by the graveyard. He reined in, had a mind to ride back, but it was cold and there was paperwork awaiting him at the office.

Will Jarrow had his mackinaw buttoned high. *One of the only places you get to rest,* he thought drily as he walked among the random scatter of graves.

The rough wooden marker at the head of the new burial place read like 'Laguna Paris Outlaw' was his whole name. Below that, it simply said: Age Unknown And May God Forgive him.

Will's face was expressionless as he looked down on the grave. He'd observed the ceremony from a shack beside the nearby creek, where the tools were kept. He wasn't going to lose any sleep over the part he'd played in sending the man to his maker. Although Laguna Paris was probably going to back-shoot the sheriff, Will still thought he could have been taken alive. He turned from the grave and walked to a short run of picket fencing where his buckskin was tied. *How much longer have you got, Sheriff?* he wondered, pulling himself up into the saddle. *For someone with your fears and suspicions, I'd suggest an alternative employ. If it's the dark, don't go out at night. Or, don't turn away from a gun-packing drunk.*

7

'Are you enjoying the book, Mr Jarrow?' April Winney asked.

'I'd say that what I've read so far was good enough.'

'Hmm, that's not quite the same thing.' April gave a small, uncertain smile. 'So what is it you don't like?'

'Nothing in particular. Truth be told, I didn't come to Blue Wells to read a book.'

'What did you come here for, then?'

A wry smile in return was just about the only answer that Will could come up with at that moment. He was slightly troubled because the girl had asked such a precise question, and he couldn't return an honest answer. And it was his own fault for implying there was a reason for him being there.

'I'm sorry, I didn't mean to pry. It's none of my business,' April added.

'Don't worry,' he said. 'It's a natural and neighbourly enough question.'

'Well if it's anything to do with what happened last night, I'm told the sheriff owes you his life. Now, that's something that is the business of the whole town.'

Will took a breath and cursed inwardly. Townsfolk had stopped him on the street to congratulate him for the part he'd played in the Chuckwalla drama. Of course they weren't aware that Will had no plan or intention to actually save the neck of Rufus Stone. He'd been short enough already with a lot of them, but didn't want to be the same with April.

Before he could prevaricate further, an elderly lady with an ear trumpet stepped in between them and rapped an ashplant cane against the counter.

'You said you'd have *Good Wives* here for me today. Well?' she demanded.

'The Pecos creeks are flooded, Mrs McReady,' April replied patiently. 'The stages are all delayed, but I'm hoping to have it tomorrow.'

'Huh, I'm eighty-five, young lady. Tomorrow might never get here.'

'Why not wait and see, ma'am?' Will put in.

52

'Have a look at *War and Peace* in the meantime? It's highly recommended.' When the woman turned her beady gaze on him, he wanted to add, *especially for lifers*, but thought better of it.

'Warren Peace? Never heard of him.'

'Mr Jarrow's only trying to help, Mrs McReady,' April said, suppressing a chuckle.

The woman squinted up at Will again. 'Jarrow, you say? Are you the one who saved the sheriff last night? Why didn't you say so?' She poked Will in the ribs with the ear piece of her trumpet. 'Maybe I'll read that book. You could do worse, girl,' she told April, nodding appreciatively as she left the store.

Some colour rose in April's cheeks and Will smiled. 'Deaf as a post an' sharp as a tack. She didn't get *everything* wrong,' he said. 'I actually came in to ask if there was somewhere you'd like to eat. With *me* that is. You heard what the old lady said.'

'I did, but perhaps I could do *better*.'

'Yeah, perhaps,' Will said, glancing up at the clock. 'But not likely. It's after one o' clock, now. What do you say?'

'Thank you, and yes, there is somewhere.'

Lunch at a boarding-house hostelry was an agreeable break for both of them. They talked of regular, peaceable things that had nothing to do with the Chuckwalla killing. If April had further thoughts on why Will was in Blue Wells, she didn't mention them. It wasn't until the meal was finished and they were preparing to leave that things took a less cheery turn when Oleg Halstrom showed up and introduced himself.

Halstrom was the editor of the *Basin Bugle*, and after a story about what had happened the previous night. But Will was staying silent, and although disappointed, Halstrom dropped the subject to pick up on something not entirely unrelated.

'I've been digging around, and come up with a troubling piece of news,' he said. 'Would either of you believe, particularly you, Miss April, that Rufus Stone has shot dead thirteen men since arriving in Blue Wells? Thirteen,' he re-stated slowly, tapping the table with an ink-stained forefinger. 'Some call that the devil's dozen.'

'That's newspaper talk, Mr Halstrom, and you know it.'

'Shameful, is what thirteen is.' Halstrom glanced at Will. 'With two in the last couple of weeks, Stone's probably carried out as many legal killings as there were in the rest of the Western Territories. As a visitor in town, wouldn't you say that's a tad excessive, Mr Jarrow?'

Will shrugged. 'That's not for me to say. But if those figures are right, there's hardly going to be a queue of folk telling him so,' he said, stony-faced.

'Exactly,' Halstrom agreed. 'I think it's called, having a tiger by the tail. It's no secret that I've always been one of the sheriff's resolute supporters – huh, let's face it, we're the only ones left alive – and I believe he's been good for this town. But I'm not sure that thirteen dead men is a fitting price to pay. He's become a dinosaur, an anachronism.' Halstrom looked from April to Will. 'Goddamnit, he's got his own trophy room.'

April pushed her coffee cup to one side. 'The sheriff's always had his detractors, and for them the criticism is factual and very real. But I think what he does is for vengeance, a misguided settlement,' she said.

'Yeah. I agree. We've all been so satisfied with the end, none of us has ever really considered the means, or the whys and wherefores,' Halstrom suggested, turning again to Will. 'About two years ago, he lost his daughter to some sort of pneumonia. Apparently, the girl was all the family he had. After her death, he was quiet for some time . . . went into a shell. But when he came out, he wanted to make the world pay. That's when he took up the work of a peace officer.'

From then on, though, Will no longer saw Halstrom or heard what was being said. The soft zizzing of the man's words increased until they filled his head with a powerful roar. All that was happening was inside him, his mind's eye holding the flimsy white shape of a body being beaten to the dark, soaked ground by the wind and rain.

'Will, are you all right?'

Through the crush and chill of Will's night-mare, the voice seemed muffled and remote. Will shook his head and blinked, looked from April to Halstrom, who was staring at him in bewilderment.

'Are you all right?' April asked again. She was squeezing his hands, her face drawn with concern.

'Yeah, it's the fine fixings. I'm not used to 'em. I think I'd best get me some outside air,' he said wearily.

8

Five miles north of Chimney Peak, Miles Glasgow
and Serle Mitchum were bunkered in the lobby of
the town's deserted hotel. They were still on edge
about the two men whose paths they'd crossed
earlier. The riders had left before nightfall, but
Mitchum recognized them, knew who they were.

'The dark one was Ed McNiece,' he said. 'A contract gunny who once worked along the Old
Spanish Trail. His partner's a nasty piece o' work
named John Kress. He carries a big old Colt in one
of them army pouches, an' likes to use it. Some call
him Horehound Jack, on account he's got a real
sweet tooth.'

'So they'll be travellin' outside o' the law,'
Glasgow suggested.

'Yeah. Never been any other way for them two.'

'What do you reckon they're doin' in this neck o' the woods?'

'Lookin' for somewhere to hole up. When we showed, they probably figured we was law an' high-tailed it. Huh, considerin' their lines o' business, who'd blame 'em?'

Glasgow didn't find Mitchum's answer very convincing. They were skin and fur traders travelling through the Sacramento Mountains in search of fox and beaver, the occasional mule deer or black bear. Each was middle-aged, ordinary in appearance and deed, and Glasgow didn't see how a brace of hard cases could mistake either of them for any kind of lawman. 'So why didn't they shoot us?' he asked.

'Dunno. It's kind o' worryin',' Mitchum answered. 'Maybe they didn't like the odds.'

The old hotel's broken shutters banged, and its decaying, clapboard walls groaned against the wind that zipped through the high mountain country. Mitchum built cigarettes, while under a flickering lantern Glasgow read a newssheet he'd picked up in Palo Verde. The pair were tough, hardened old men, not used to much other company. Meeting the two riders earlier had unsettled them, made them nervous.

South of Chimney Peak, and west of the Pecos,

the Sacramentos had a reputation that discouraged most travellers. In the remote, slick-rock canyons and dry gulches there were a few men who had drifted south from Utah and Colorado to work in the copper mines near Picacho. They knew few laws and lived by even less, often married Mexican girls who crossed into New Mexico.

Mitchum and Glasgow were on their way to the timberline, but now they talked of their misgivings, the doubtful advantage of travelling through that hostile part of the wild country. Eventually both men dropped off to sleep, and neither of them heard the squeak of a rusty hinge as the side door eased open.

With a swirl of dust and wind close behind them, six shadowy figures walked quietly into the room. As they drew closer to the sleeping pair, light from the guttering lamp shimmered on their handguns. Leading the bunch were Ed McNiece and John Kress. Trying to stifle a consumptive rasp, the last man in held a kerchief close to his mouth.

'Come wake up, you lazy good for nothin's,' the copper-headed Rex Ferry shouted, clicking back the action of his Colt.

Glasgow and Mitchum jerked upright to find themselves surrounded. The twin muzzles of a shotgun prodded hard against Mitchum's cheek as he stared up into the deeply scarred and bearded face of an outlaw known as Ike Bound.

Bound grinned and shook his head. 'I'm excitable. Best you don't move,' he rasped sparely. 'Piss your pants an' I could likely pull triggers.'

Mitchum couldn't see much in the low light, but he caught the ripe, pungent animal odours. *We're in trouble*, he thought. *Hope they're not Comanchero.*

'What do you want with us boys? We ain't nothin'. Got nothin' either,' Glasgow said.

'We remember you say that,' Malachi Bound said in a similar manner to his elder brother. 'Who wants to see the night critters we find?' he called out, as a gaunt, chalky-featured spectre of a man wearing a faded linen duster stepped into the pool of yellow light.

Mitchum blinked and his jaw dropped a fraction. 'Eels Painter,' he gasped in surprise. 'You're a ways off trail. I thought your particular huntin' ground was closer to the San Antonios.'

'Hell, Eels, you're more famous than we thought,' Malachi Bound said. 'Us too, I reckon,' he added with a foolish grin.

The elder Bound stepped back, allowing Painter to jab Mitchum with the barrel of a Winchester rifle. 'What you all doin' this far south?'

'We're trappers . . . deal in animal skins. Where

else do we goddamn work?' Mitchum retorted. 'There's two o' you here might've guessed that.'

'Guessin' ain't our game,' John Kress answered, before swallowing a plug of sugar candy.

'We've got notes . . . bills o' sale,' Glasgow said, indicating his saddle-bags.

'Lawmen always got some kind o' papers,' intoned the wraith-like Painter.

Mitchum and Glasgow exchanged an incredulous stare 'Lawmen?' they replied in unison. 'We been given some strange names in our time, but never lawmen,' Mitchum said. 'Certainly not in the last ten or fifteen years.'

McNiece bared his teeth, his mud-coloured eyes shifting from Mitchum to Glasgow to Painter. 'Only a snaky star-toter would ride up here knowin' we was in camp,' he suggested.

'We didn't know you were here,' Glasgow contributed with a tinge of fear. 'We usually go places where there ain't any folk.'

'Yeah. Swear to God that's what we do,' Mitchum agreed eagerly, but with the thought that: *if the smell's anything to go by, we've been lured to the right place.* He looked Painter straight in the eye, wondered if the same thoughts were going through his mind. 'You believe that, don't you?' he added, as close to innocent-sounding as he could get.

Grimacing from the pain in his chest, Painter gestured for Ike Bound to fetch him a chair. Muttering curses, he set his rifle aside and set himself down, the lamplight breaking across his pallid face.

There were aspects of decay and decline in the old man, but it was clear he was boss of the outfit. 'See what they got,' he ordered, then hawked and spat in the direction of Glasgow.

The two men under guard were searched, the outlaws quickly coming up with a ninety-dollar take. 'Small peas,' Ferry sneered.

'Mountain men . . . trappers . . . wolfers,' Painter stated coldly. 'Since when do men who sell furs carry such few dollars?'

'When the goddamn free trappin's nearly all gone. That's when,' Mitchum explained testily. 'Besides, what we do have is salted. We wouldn't carry a poke just to get robbed of it, would we?'

Ferry waved his Colt as if he was impatient to use it. 'You sayin' we steal your miserable dollars? You insultin' us?' he menaced.

'No, but open doors tempt saints. Ain't no one but a fool says otherwise,' Mitchum retorted. He looked to Painter as if for support, but didn't find it.

Eels Painter wasn't the old man's real name. Eels

was a simple ape on nature, but he stole Painter like most everything else he'd ever come by. He'd been born George Paris, but dropped George and tacked on Painter, after dodgers with his name on them started to circulate in the lowlands. He'd seen the title on a signboard outside of a store in Elkins.

Old Eels had killed a lot of men in his time, but few knew it. He was a legend of the southern Sacramentos who, in keeping to his own country, avoided the dangers of the Goodnight-Loving trail and Butterfield Stage Line. Justly feared in the numberless canyons and mountain valleys, he'd been dying since a doctor had diagnosed advanced tuberculosis, giving him six months to live. His lungs were shredded, but until his time came he had little else to do and nowhere to go.

'Smell ain't right,' he grated at length, slowly tapping the side of his waxen nose. 'Law smell.'

A bigger fear started to squeeze at Glasgow and Mitchum. What Painter was saying amounted to a death sentence. The trappers could be shot dead, and only the vultures would ever know what became of them. For a good fifty miles north and south of the border with Mexico, lots of folk went missing.

Once again, Mitchum got to thinking it was too

bad they hadn't thought of that before. Stirred into action, he jumped to his feet. But both Ferry and Kress were waiting for such a move, and Ferry swatted him down with a crack from the barrel of his Colt.

Blood oozed from Mitchum's split lip and Glasgow stared at him with fearful eyes. 'That's what they want, Serle,' he said. 'Think o' some other way to show we ain't John Law.'

Painter sunk further down into his chair, sighed and smiled tiredly. 'Like Mr an' Mrs Cuffy playin' in their den,' he rumbled out, as Mitchum and Glasgow squabbled nervously.

The man once known as George Paris enjoyed any sort of fight because it meant life – the one thing that he was fast running out of. His wife was dead, his son was on the drift again and all he had left now was his gang. They were all loyal enough, but it was his own flesh and blood he wanted to bring him comforts in the final days. He knew there was too much of himself in his son. The boy wasn't content to follow like McNiece and Kress and the others. No, he had to keep going off alone, trying to prove he was his father's son and deadly equal.

The chalky skin of Painter's old face wilted. He'd spent most of his years as a mean, vicious son-of-a-bitch, his family life full of mistakes and misunderstandings. It never appeared that he thought much of his rebellious boy, but he did. He cared deeply for his Mexican wife, too, but even she had died without really knowing it.

The young Laguna had grown up believing his pa considered him an unworthy heir to his legendary reputation. Sadly, the old man never had the words or the wit to persuade him otherwise. The two of them quarrelled and patched up, only to quarrel again. They were forever competing, but in the trackless wastes of the Sacramentos, George Paris was kingfish, his handsome, blue-eyed son the wounded contender. Paradoxically, every time Laguna left to make his name some other place, the old man missed him with a ferocious longing. And every time the boy came back, they fought like cat and dog.

Eels Painter coughed into his kerchief. Then he looked at the two men who were waiting for him to make up his mind about what to do with Mitchum and Glasgow.

'So where's their guns?' he asked, as though to no one in particular. 'What do they carry?'

Realizing they hadn't located any side arms, his men looked uncertainly at one another.

'They got none hidden. There's knives . . . nothin' more,' Malachi Bound said.

'You want us to take a closer look?' Ferry asked with mean intent.

'Yeah, do that,' Painter answered indifferently.

Ferry and Bound checked out the saddle-bags again, intolerantly tossed personal doodads across the floor. A folded news-sheet slewed towards Painter and he jabbed it with the heel of his boot.

'You satisfied?' Mitchum choked out. 'Fingerin' through our drawers an' doodads. We got a couple of old pieces tied across the mules. You want to go take a look?'

Ferry narrowed his eyes. He looked disappointed, not sure what to do next. He was ready to dole out punishment for little more reason than the captives looked and sounded different to him.

'Huh, lawmen who don't carry guns,' Painter sneered. 'Times really are changin'.'

You're a curious mix, Mitchum thought to himself. *Bright and dim at the same time.*

The outlaws looked frustrated, as though their fun and games had suddenly ended. But Mitchum and Glasgow saw a chance.

'You believe us now? We're trappers, mountain men, goddamnit . . . how many more times?' Glasgow shouted in frustration, his face sheened with nervous sweat. 'We don't have gunfights. We use them old squirrellers for knockin' varmints out o' trees.'

'Yeah, I've just got to believe that,' Painter conceded. 'An' you've likely been sellin' 'em to my people as kit beaver. Who'd expect to get cheated by lawmen?'

Glasgow and Mitchum gulped in frustration. Painter's men took to eager smirking once again. They'd ridden in with the prospect of cruel fun, and now it was beginning to look like they'd get it.

Ike Bound brandished his shotgun snake-like at Glasgow's head. 'Finger still wants to work,' he rasped, anticipating a nod from his boss.

But Painter was in an unexpectedly merciful mood. 'We don't wan't 'em comin' back here preyin' on honest, God-fearin' folk. Huh, next time they'd probably wear their goddamn shiny badges. Give 'em a lesson they won't forget,' was his judgement. 'You won't need your irons for that. Put 'em away,' he added with an appropriate gesture.

Ike Bound looked contented enough as he hauled Mitchum to his feet, started smacking his head from side to side with a hard, open hand. His younger brother and Rex Ferry set about toe-poking Glasgow as he tried to gather in his personal possessions.

McNiece and Kress didn't join in. They were hired gunnies who regarded themselves as a cut above the others. They looked on, but found little interest in the treatment being meted out to Mitchum and Glasgow. Kress was urging Ike Bound to put some muscle into what he was doing when he was distracted by a strange choking sound from behind him. In the same instant he realized that for a few minutes there had been nothing other than silence from Eels Painter.

He turned to see the old man leaning forward in his chair clutching the news-sheet. His eyes were staring fixedly, his jaw was working and he was breathing heavy as he scanned the lamplit pages.

'Eels!' Ferry yelled with anxiety, stepping quickly to Painter's side. 'What's ailin' you, Boss? Is it the 'sumption?'

The small gang lived in fear of the day when the sickness would put their leader in the ground. They knew full well that without Painter's canny senses and leadership, they'd make easy game for those who hunted them.

But it wasn't Painter's health that was taking him bad. It was the printed words of the news-sheet he'd trapped under his boot. Held between his shaking hands it was difficult for McNiece and

Kress to read, but they could make out the head-line:

Outlaw Laguna Paris
Killed by Blue Wells Lawman.

There was a sudden fade of the violent slapping and grunting when Ike and Malachi Bound real-ized there was something seriously wrong. Leaving Mitchum and Glasgow semi-conscious from their battering, they hurried across the room. Ed McNiece took the news-sheet from Painter's twitching hands and read aloud:

' "Sheriff Stone's report makes it clear that law and order will be maintained. The dead outlaw was almost certainly seeking to avenge his former outlaw partner Cory Newton." '

'Hell, Eels. You warned the boy to stay away from that lizard tail,' Ferry seethed in disgust.

But Painter was up on his feet, still looking the colour of death, although not trembling any more. It was as though he was taking in a draught of reju-venating physic to banish the weakness from his limbs and the rotting of his lungs. Within moments, he looked and sounded almost like the old George Paris, making a blunt Comanche gesture that meant death.

'I've heard o' this man Stone,' he said, pausing to draw in a deep breath, refusing to cough. 'He's livin' on borrowed time.'

Mitchum and Glasgow were back to standing, rubbing their faces, watching and wondering what effect this turn of events might hold for them. They were alarmed by the set of Painter's pale face, sensing a mistaken look or word would seal their fate.

'An' so I know what to do . . . where it's to be done,' he rasped. 'Let's go.'

For half an hour, the trappers hardly moved. They gathered up their belongings, raised weary smiles in trying to recall when they'd been in a like predicament. By the time they dared take a look outside of the deserted hotel, Painter was long gone.

The gang rode swiftly through the night, along dark trails with which they were so familiar. The old man rode ahead, tears from the knife-edged wind riving his stony features. But he felt stronger, tougher now than he had in years, curiously reassured that it took the death of his son to get him so roused.

9

Rufus Stone paused in his paperwork. He listened to the sound of footsteps outside his office, glancing up as a shadow moved across the doorway. Moments later he heard the porch rocker scrape on the boardwalk then creak as it slowly started to rock to and fro.

Deputy Eben Gent, seated by the stove warming his hands, made to rise, but Stone motioned him to stay put. It was midday, but so darkly overcast that the overhead lamps were already lit. The glow faintly illuminated the gallery of dead badmen which lined the wall behind the desk. The latest additions showed Cory Newton with his hands clutched around the butt of a Dragoon's Colt. Roped to a circuit photographer's plank, Laguna

71

Paris was stripped to the waist. Clearly visible was the big, single bullet hole in the middle of his chest.

All the photographs made Gent ill at ease, although he never dared say so. If Stone had ornamented the office with Navaho rugs or cow horns, he would have accepted it. As it was, he was an unsophisticated young man and lived in both awe and fear of the Blue Wells sheriff.

Stone returned to his writing of incident reports. He had a well-practised, single-minded approach to such tally work, but the insidious squeak of the rocker continued to distract him. He jabbed the pen in the ink pot and leaned back in the chair for a full minute, listening motionless.

'Shall I go see what he wants, Sheriff?' Gent asked, breaking the silence. 'He sure ain't out there sunnin' himself.'

'No.'

Gent scratched his head. 'It seems to me it would be a lot easier an' safer to get your attention by knockin' on the door.'

'Yeah, that's what I've been thinkin',' Stone muttered thoughtfully.

The sheriff was as puzzled as anybody else as to why Will Jarrow continued to hang around Blue Wells. He had no gainful employ, regularly visited the mercantile's book section, and made use of two saloons. Who or what the hell was he watching, or waiting for?

Stone was beginning to think that Will Jarrow was watching him, and it was starting to abrade his nerves. It had already occurred to him that the man might be somebody with a grudge against him waiting for his chance to strike. After all, there'd been a few of them. But to balance the thinking, Jarrow had actually saved him from being gunned down by Laguna Paris.

Stone lifted his head when the rocker stopped squeaking. He waited, then a moment later the sound started again. He cursed silently, got to his feet and pulled his Spencer from the rack. He knew how to handle a Colt, but the .52 carbine could be a more convincing ally. He didn't anticipate needing or using it against Jarrow, but he rarely left his office without it. He never knew when the next killer would ride into town seeking him out, and he wanted to be good and ready. In reality, he welcomed them as an additional benefit of his job, an earned entertainment.

His steely gaze went over the photographs as he adjusted the fit of his hat. There was space on his walls for more, and he knew there almost certainly would be. His reputation drew glory hunters and vengeance seekers in equal measure. As they came he would kill them, and until the town finally sickened of it.

A thinking crease showed between his eyes as he glanced at the latest copy of the *Basin Bugle*. For the first time, its editor, Oleg Halstrom, had chosen to comment on the sheriff's death count. Stone was surprised it had taken so long, but now the publication had raised the issue of the lengthy list, he anticipated that it wouldn't be long before others took up the concern. From the beginning, there had been an element who questioned his hard-nosed methods, but they were persistent malcontents and of little consequence. Those who referred to him as 'Stone Dead' or 'Heart of Stone', did so with a certain proud humour, secure that they had a strong man watching out for them. But once someone with a voice sat down and began to dwell on what law and order was costing in terms of human life, Stone knew there would be a swell of unrest.

Fortunately, he reckoned he was as capable of handling civic unrest and editorial criticism as he was of taking out gunmen and troublesome drifters.

Now, he half smiled as he stepped from his office onto the boardwalk. He was recalling a quip

74

about the town's wood yard being renamed 'The Bone Box Company', due to its output of casket timber.

Will Jarrow was gently rocking to and fro as he watched the street. He didn't turn at the sound of Stone's boots, nor look up when the sheriff's tall figure halted close by the chair.

'What is it you want, Jarrow?' Stone demanded.

The rocker stopped and Will glanced up. 'Sheriff,' he said, with a spread of his hands. 'I'm just sitting here not wanting for anything at the moment.'

'Your manner's irkin' me, Jarrow. An' I'm wondering why you'd want to do that?'

Will's hazel eyes followed the progress of a battered old mud wagon being driven towards Sourdough Weems's livery stables. 'No need to fuss yourself, Sheriff,' he answered levelly. 'I'm a hard-working feller who's got himself a mite tuckered, an' I'm taking a short vacation. I hear that's real fashionable out East.'

'So where've you been workin' to get this *tuckered*?'

'Here an' there.'

'That's the sort o' crack I get when I question men with doubtful pasts. I reckon there's some sort o' vagrancy order I could take you in for.'

75

'Have you got suspicions about me, Sheriff?'

'For someone with such a goddamn slippery tongue? Yeah, you could say that.'

Will created a tolerant half-smile. 'This might come as a surprise, but there's not an outlaw hiding behind every ball of tumbleweed. Not even west of the Pecos.'

The conversation was interrupted by two snarling and snapping mangy dogs that had chased a rat or like critter under the stubby pilings of the boardwalk. Stone stamped his foot and growled a challenge, took the opportunity for a probing look at Will.

'We'll beg to differ on that,' he said. 'An' I'm not forgettin' the debt I owe you,' he added with little-sounding sincerity.

'There's no one in my debt, Sheriff. Certainly not *you*.'

Stone took a deep breath. 'I'm beginnin' to sense there's somethin' personal goin' on here, Jarrow. You should know I'm a simple man, an' not a good one to mess with,' he warned.

Will stared up at him directly, his tone now harder. 'An' *you* should know I'm not someone who scares easy. Bullying this soft, undemanding town's one thing. Tryin' it on *me*'s another.'

Suddenly, feeling like Will Jarrow was closing on

an inner, concealed trouble, the sheriff's manner darkened. For the first time since they'd met, he was a tad troubled. 'Are you sure there ain't somethin' you got on your chest, young feller?'

Will got up, flexing his shoulders then his fingers. 'If there is something going on, Sheriff, it doesn't include me riding from this or any other town just because somebody with a badge reckons I should. Does that make sense?'

Stone smacked the side of his leg with the barrel of the carbine. 'Listen to me, Jarrow. If you don't tell me what the hell it is you're wantin' from this town, where you been or where the hell you're goin', I'm goin' to give you billy hell an' then some. Does *that* make sense?'

'You've got to have grounds, Sheriff, and you really don't. You can't do much with me legally, because I've not yet done nothing *illegal*. We're all innocent of crimes until proven guilty.'

A small, dawning smile broke across Stone's hard face. 'Yeah, an' the guilty ones always run. You know what I think, Jarrow? You're so goddamn shifty of where you've been and not been, so able to live within yourself, it's breakin' as clear as day.'

'What is, Sheriff?'

'You're jailmeat. Yuma or Fort Wingate. Amarillo, Texas, even.'

77

'Well, if ever I was, my time's served, an' my conscience is clear,' Will returned. 'Could you say the same, Sheriff? Have you done time for all those wrongs, all those crimes *you've* committed?'

'What the hell are you meanin'?'

'Haven't you got something that keeps you awake at nights? Not just the men you've put under the ground, but something locked away in your mind that you can never think on without doubt or question?'

Stone drew back a pace, felt a rill of icy sweat touch the small of his back. His fingers squeezed the breech of his carbine as though it were the flesh around Will Jarrow's neck. He was now in little doubt regarding the menace of the man. But why, and for what? A moment later, he was relieved when the telegraph operator arrived with a wire from Santa Fe, and he heard his name being called. It provided him with an excuse to curse, turn away and step hurriedly back into the office.

Standing by his desk, Rufus Stone stared back out through the window, watched uneasily as Will stepped down to the hard-packed dirt of the street. Then he read the telegraphed message which contained routine information about an impending court case. Both he and the observant deputy were surprised to see that his hands carried a slight tremble.

10

Will Jarrow walked through Blue Wells in an irritated, dissatisfied mood. In his eyes, the town's outward appearance supported a flourishing confidence. Nothing would be allowed to disturb that too much, not even the occasional blast of gunfire consigning another soul to its bleak graveyard.

But Will didn't want the wholesome calm. He wanted the turmoil of unrest, the hue and cry of a fight. For these were the conditions under which he'd get his edge, when Rufus Stone was more likely to make a mistake. *Yeah, sooner or later*, he thought. *It will happen. It's the way of all things.* Except he'd already waited too long, and the possibility seemed no closer than it had when he'd first arrived.

Through dust-cleared windows, he glanced into

the stores, at affluent storekeepers waiting on well-turned-out customers. A gleaming blood bay stood quietly in front of the Chuckwalla Saloon and for a moment Will considered sharing a simon-pure whiskey with one of the girls. Back across the street, a Dearborn awaited the emergence of a rancher from the cattlemen's bank. Will would have bet cash money they'd all lodge a vote for Rufus Stone's next election, doubtless turn in that night believing they'd done their bit for respectability and civic improvement.

A couple of boardwalk idlers watched him with curiosity, making quiet remarks after he'd passed by. Will Jarrow had become quite a talking point in their town. The sheriff wasn't the only one who found his continuing presence and lack of any useful service curious. Someone had actually asked April Winney what she knew about him. She'd answered by telling them he was a thoughtful and polite man, whose company she enjoyed. As for any mystery about his past, well that was for April to know, and for her alone as fascinating as a closed book.

Will turned off the main street, continuing his walk to the north end of town. He reached Carlo's Jug, where he'd recently spoken to a homesteader named Hector Speke. The man had interested him because he too had run up against the wilful malice of Rufus Stone. But this was a different story.

It seemed a neighbouring rancher's cow had turned up on Speke's claimed land. Stone had got wind of it, and instead of accepting the animal as a stray, had hauled him in on charges that were tantamount to rustling. Speke was cleared, but mud had stuck. Furthermore, the incident caused him to miss a loan payment and the bank concerned was threatening to close out his account. Will had asked why the man hadn't taken action against Stone for wrongful arrest.

'Face up in the alfalfa's better than face down in the Pecos,' had been Speke's measured reply.

Now, two days later, Will returned to the dog hole, where he ordered a shot of Carlo's finest. He gulped as the raw corn scorched his stomach, then signalled for another. He glanced around, nodded at Hector Speke who was watching him from a gloomy corner. He carried his glass across to the table and pulled out a chair.

'It's said that men who drink alone have a problem,' Will offered with a considerate smile. 'I saw your rig outside, but thought you'd be long gone.'

Speke looked up and nodded passively. 'Yeah, so

did I.' He swilled the cheap whiskey around his glass. 'It's kind o' hard to leave with any real purpose, when you realize there ain't no particular place to go.'

The man had been brought down, but Will suspected there might still be a dash of vinegar. 'What's in your pot?' he asked.

'Nothin'. Huh, there never was much, an' then the bottom fell out. By the time I paid up what I owed . . . seed, ploughshares an' stuff, I couldn't even piss in it.'

Leaning back, Will shoved a hand into his pants pocket and drew out a fold of notes. He took two tens and discreetly pushed them across the table in his fist.

'That wasn't a plea for a handout,' Speke said.

'I know, and it's not. I just don't want you suffering at the hands of Rufus Stone, if I can do anything about it.'

'Why's it of concern to you? Is there somethin' you're not tellin' me?'

'Maybe. But right now, that's not important. What I'm handing over is an advance. An advance on damages you can get awarded when you take Stone to court. Look on it as a kind of grubstake.'

'You reckon a court's goin' to find for *me*?'

'Listen, Speke, we're not livin' in the dark ages

any more. You can *prove* that your being locked up on a rustling charge – a charge that was later dismissed – lost you your livelihood *and* your good name. The town can't have it both ways. If its people want to make civic progress, it's got to support you. It's their law as well as yours. We could go see a lawyer and ask them?'

Thoughtful and tempted, Speke fingered the money. 'You talk o' the town, but it's not *them*, an' you know it. What do you know about the law?'

'I know that if you don't use it, Stone wins. You want that?'

'No. But he don't take kindly to men goin' up against him.'

'That's because they use a gun. You take him to court, and I'll stand by you either way.'

Speke's cheerless eyes narrowed. 'You really want him', don't you? I saw that the other day. Now I can feel it. Tell me what it is?'

This was risky ground for Will and he knew it. For weeks he'd kept secret his feelings towards Stone. But regrettably he was now being forced to open up with stuff he'd wanted kept hidden. He'd hoped to sit back and wait for a situation where he could intervene, work to bring the sheriff down. There had been a moment when if he had kept quiet, Stone would have been grinding at knots in

Chuckwalla's floor. But as Will mumbled sardonically into his whiskey that night, it would have been a much too swift and dignified death. Laguna Paris's fated involvement had actually caught him unawares.

Yeah, there's a pile of hurt and suffering to go yet, he was thinking when Speke brought him from the dark reverie. 'Sorry,' he grunted, swallowing on the bile. 'Must be Carlo's double-rectified.'

Hector Speke didn't get the joke. He had little humour nowadays, but as Will anticipated, a pinch of grit still remained.

'I'll do it. Why should he get away with ruinin' me on account he's got a big gun an' a big goddamn badge?' the smallholder said emotionally.

Will nodded. 'It's the bigger they come,' he encouraged. 'Just keep that in mind.'

Ten minutes later, after one more round of Carlo's corn, the pair were on their way to see if Attorney Euple Daggert was available.

By the time Hector Speke walked into the boarding-house with Will Jarrow that night, everybody seemed to know that he had instigated legal action against the sheriff. It was also known that Attorney Daggert believed Speke had a reasonable to good chance of success. What wasn't known was that it was Will Jarrow who was financing the action, or how it was affecting Sheriff Stone.

Ignoring the stares and questions of the customers, Will and Speke dined earnestly on steak and potatoes. They ended their meal with coffee, after which Speke went very quiet. He stifled a yawn, and Will presumed it was a combination of lack of air and nerves. He advised Speke to turn in and get himself a good night's sleep. He said if there was anything to answer for, he would deal with it.

'Are you supportin' ol' Hector, Mr Jarrow?'

'Is that true, you an' the sheriff had words this morning, Mr Jarrow?'

'You figure Speke can secure a conviction against Sheriff Stone for unlawful arrest, Mr Jarrow?'

Will made vague, noncommittal responses. He thought he'd made progress today and was satisfied to let it go at that. It was Stone's reaction he was interested in, the thought that if the man was pushed he might do something imprudent.

Shortly, he walked to the office of the *Basin Bugle*. From the front windows, he could keep an eye on the jailhouse while he talked to Oleg Halstrom.

The newspaper editor wanted to know all about the pending court action, but again, Will played down his involvement. 'I'm simply advising on the law of it,' he said.

'Is that it at last? You're a lawyer?' Halstrom was making another attempt to ferret out something on Will's background.

'I've picked up bits of book law in my time. Just found a place for some of it to come in handy, I guess. Hah, do I look like an attorney?'

'Not necessarily,' the newsman conceded. 'But then, you don't look much like owl hoot either.'

Will looked at him sharply. 'Why should I? Has Stone been talking to you?'

Halstrom nodded. 'You'll probably find out anyway. He was here earlier. He wants to use my contacts to see if I can dig up some background on you. He seems to have it in his head that you're a fugitive . . . some sort of public enemy.'

With a long-suffering smile, Will looked diagonally across the street to the jailhouse. 'Do you ever read the Holy Book?' he asked.

'Yeah, it's been known. Why'd you ask?'

'You know where it says, "Let him without guilt throw the first stone"?'

'I've heard of a saying that's something like that.'

'Well, it seems to me, your good sheriff's going around pitching rocks as if he's got something to prove and only a short time to do it.'

Halstrom was suddenly more interested in where the conversation was going. 'Are you saying Stone's guilty of something ... got something to hide?' he asked.

'Well, most of us have got that. What do you know about his background?' Will knew he was treading dangerous ground, but couldn't help it. The edgy disposition that had been with him most of the day was still there.

Halstrom gestured towards his filing cabinets. 'Plenty. That stuff can be meat an' potatoes when there's nothing else. But then, Rufus Stone has lived most of his life under a highlight. His credentials are faultless wherever he's been employed.'

'That's as a lawman ... a town sheriff. What about his private life? What readers are really interested in.' Will's face looked taut and hard as he scrutinized the editor. 'What, for instance, do you know about his family? What have you got on them?'

'I know he lost a daughter in Santa Rosa about two years ago. It hit him hard. Most folk know that, though.'

88

'Do you know how she died? Or why?'

'I think it was pneumonia.'

'You don't just up and die of pneumonia. Most folk know that as well.'

Halstrom gave Will's response a few moments' thought. 'I do recollect there was something strange. Apparently, the girl wandered off, but it was during one of the worst storms in years. A search party went out from Santa Rosa, but they found her too late. She never recovered. But why do I get the feeling that you know all that?' the editor added with an enquiring look.

'You're a newsman. Maybe you've got a nose for these things. And maybe like me, you've learnt it's safer to only ask questions you know the answer to,' Will suggested. 'And that's still only *how*, not *why*. For instance, did you know that the night of that big storm, the girl was due to meet up with a man she'd fallen in love with, that they were planning to run off? Stone did. So he dragged her to her room and locked her in . . . turned the key on his own daughter. Did you know that?'

'No. I'd have remembered. Where did you get it from?'

'That don't matter. But it's the goddamn truth of it, and *that does*.' Will almost snarled out the words.

As a newspaper editor, it was incumbent upon Halstrom to enquire more. But Will had said his piece. He had turned his back, was already walking for the door.

Beyond the main street, six strangers on weary, sweat-stained horses had a sideways glance as they slowly rode past the tented sides of Carlo's Jug.

11

Sheriff Stone was preparing to take a turn of the street. Eben Gent had signed off an hour earlier, and he was alone in the jailhouse. He rubbed the toes of his boots against the back of his legs and shined his badge on a cuff of his coat. As he reached for his hat, the scrape of a hesitant step sounded on his porch. In a single, smooth action, he swung the barrel of his big carbine to cover the door.

Most late visitors were greeted in this way, and Stone never apologized for scaring them. That was his advantage. On two occasions since he'd arrived in Blue Wells, would-be killers had come calling at the jailhouse. They'd failed in their missions, of course, but only because of his hostile vigilance.

'Come in,' he called when the knock came.

The door opened and a spectre with fevered eyes stood there, the darkness framing him. He was spattered in light mud, wind-blown and illusory.

'Jeeesus H,' Stone cursed. 'Are you sure you got the right place, mister?'

Without reply, the man entered. Despite his emaciated frame, the sheriff saw in the apparition a certain flinty dignity. Keeping the carbine raised, he moved aside, even though the man didn't look capable of stabbing a mutton chop.

The man held every ounce of Stone's attention as he looked around, as his eyes took in the dead man's gallery that ornamented the wall behind the desk.

'If an' when they send the old Reaper down, I guess he'll look like you,' Stone said. 'You ain't him, are you, feller?'

'The name's Painter,' the man replied. 'You won't have heard o' me.'

Stone anxiously searched his mental files, but no such name or unique appearance came to mind. As luck would have it, there was no such document on Eels Painter – previously George Paris – of the Sacramento Mountains. Now, an unprecedented event had drawn the old man from the safety of his mountain hideaway, near to halfway across the state of New Mexico.

'What can I do for you, Mr Painter?' Stone asked, lowering the barrel of the carbine.

'I'm lookin' for my boy.'

'What's his name?'

'Boy.'

'Boy Painter? Name don't ring a bell. When did he go missing?'

'A while back.' Painter walked closer to the wall behind the desk where the lampshade threw some of the pictures into shadow. 'Sure would be a shock to see your own kinfolk nailed up here,' he said quietly.

'Yeah, I guess it would. Especially if they'd murdered an innocent man, woman or child. You're looking at the mortal likenesses of scum, Mr Painter. They're not meant to shock a decent, God-fearing man.'

But Painter wasn't one of those men. He was cruelly shaken by one of the most recent pictures, even though he'd been forewarned. He'd come alone to see for himself, because he had to be sure.

His son had been photographed in an upright position, stripped of his vest to show the massive damage of a .52 Spencer carbine. The weight of the body was supported by ropes tied in loops around the plank. Laguna Paris's once bright-blue eyes were closed, but his mouth was twisted as though in surprise. A revolver had been shoved into his waistband. It was the Navy Colt that Painter had given him to observe his majority. Tacked at his side was a faded reward poster that linked him to Cory Newton and a wretched two-bit robbery.

Some mountain men said that Eels Painter was running with the devil, that if he was all human the lung disease would have eaten him alive, many moons ago. But in union with the devil or not, this picture of his son skewered his soul. He stood motionless for so long that Stone asked him if there was something wrong.

Painter shut his eyes and took a long, shallow, rasping breath. It took a few seconds, then his bony face turned to the big sheriff. 'Just takin' a moment. I'm no longer in the pink o' condition, if you hadn't noticed.'

'There's a chair here if you want it.'

Painter shook his head. 'Sure is some display you got here, Sheriff,' he indicated, jabbing a thumb at the pictures.

'They serve a purpose. A reminder to any man of what to expect if he breaks the law in my town.' Stone frowned slightly. 'Is there anything . . . something else, Mr Painter?'

'No, don't seem like it,' Painter said. 'Perhaps some other time,' he added emotionlessly, turning back to the door. *Ain't no 'perhaps' about it, you butcherin' son-of-a-bitch,* he thought, stepping to the boardwalk.

By the time Stone came out to begin his patrol, Eels Painter was gone, disappeared back into the darkness.

12

'It's busy tonight,' Will Jarrow said, taking a look around the Chuckwalla.

'Yes, it is. Includes a few new faces, though.'

'Word must have got round you're working that side of the bar.'

'I don't know quite what you mean by that, but I'm thinking it's some sort of compliment,' Grace Chard said with a smile.

'Yeah. Not one of my obvious qualities. But as long as *I* know what I mean.'

Grace leaned an elbow on the bar and smiled again. 'Perhaps you should work at it. You know the first day you walked in, I thought: here's someone who watches all he says, and does so for fear of giving something away. And that's me thinking *I* know what *I* mean. You don't mind me saying,

96

do you, Will?'

Will shook his head. 'No, not a bit. What's sauce for the goose, eh? So, while we're on such familiar terms, why does a girl like you spend time mixing with a man they call Rufus Heart of Stone?'

Grace stiffened instantly. 'That's got nothing to do with familiarity. Except *too much*,' she said huffily. 'It's intrusive, Will, and none of your business.'

'I wondered *why* because it's usually grief in the long run. You must know that, Grace?'

'Yes, I do,' she snapped and walked away.

'There's something else I've got to work at,' Will muttered. He sipped his drink, thinking he knew what lay ahead for Grace. She was infatuated with the sheriff, and Will didn't want to see her harmed too badly when the man went down. *There's got to be some other way of telling her,* he thought wryly. But Grace Chard was of a trusting nature. She would stick close, whatever, and Will lifted his glass in a silent toast. A moment later, he turned to see the big man himself push a shoulder through the batwings. *It's called timing,* was Will's next ironic thought.

Stone's arrival never went unnoticed, and there was a brief pause in the saloon's general activity. Nearly everyone swung a cursory glance at Stone, who was taking his usual imposing position just inside the door. Nearly everyone, that is, not all.

From various quarters of the room, there were new faces who continued to watch keenly as the sheriff made his way confidently towards the bar.

Five of these newcomers were within easy reach of the back side door. There was a heavily built, darkly featured man seated at a poker layout. Off to his left, leaning against a wall, was a man who carried a big pouch holster and Colt. Leaning on the upright piano, chewing on a soda cracker while closely watching Rufus Stone, was a man with a high-waisted gunbelt. A tall man with a beard and deeply scarred face stood next to him. Closest to the back end of the bar was another stranger, a copper-headed youngster with a revolver concealed beneath his coat. The five had arrived at dusk, together with the ashen-faced man in a faded duster, who now sat alone at a table close to the front.

There had been others at the table when the frail, coughing man took his seat, but one by one they had moved away. It could have been his blood-flecked kerchief and ghostly pallor that prompted them to leave the table. Then again it could have been the chilling eyes that scared them off.

Stone nodded to Grace, scowled at the back of Will, who was now watching him in the back-bar mirror.

'Hello, Rufus.' Grace said, as usual putting a warmer quality to her voice. 'Is this the evening for a little measure of something?'

'Hah. As well you know, Grace, I've never been tempted with a little anythin', except peace.' The Blue Wells lawman rarely drank and didn't take tobacco, indulged in very few – if any – of life's luxuries. He smiled and turned his attention to Will. 'I hear you've been monkeyin' with the law, Mr Jarrow,' he said. 'You ought to be careful. You know what they say about a little monkeyin' bein' a dangerous thing.'

Will gave Stone a deadpan look. He was going to correct him with, 'It's knowledge', but he knew the sheriff was fully aware of the words he'd chosen. The rapport that had been established between them following the Laguna Paris incident had long since evaporated. In his mulish way, Stone had been obliged, but had soon discovered that Will Jarrow wasn't interested. He'd become a bellyache, a burr under the blanket.

Stone was referring to the Hector Speke situation. He might not like the fact that Speke was within his rights in bringing about court action, but he was going to have to accept it.

'That's what's good about due legal process; it has to be seen to be done,' Will replied, guessing that Stone would resent the intervention of any outsider.

'Are you sure you won't have that drink, Rufus?' Grace asked, an anxious frown going from one man to the other.

Stone shook his head. He was concentrating on Will, but taking in the fact that from around the room, a handful of men were steadily watching him.

'I hear you've also been talkin' to Editor Halstrom,' he said. His voice was a bit softer, but no friendlier for it.

'Yeah,' Will conceded. Now he looked flatly at the sheriff. 'There are some things I know more about than he does. And he's a newsman. Makes sense.'

'Are you trying to start a fight?' Grace tried to defuse the situation with a laugh. 'Lordy, if anybody should be friends, it's you two.'

'Fight?' broke in a familiar voice. 'If it's a fight you're wantin' you'd best climb into my goddamn chops.' The pain-wracked face of Sourdough Weems emerged from a group of nearby drinkers. Fighting took his mind off most anything else, and

100

he was always ready to cultivate it when he could. 'Hah,' he snorted derisively, looking from Stone to Will. 'That wouldn't be a fight, sonny. It would be one o' the sheriff's Texas breakfasts.'

'Shut up!' Will, Stone and Grace shouted back in unison. But their remonstration had little effect. If people weren't ganging up on the irascible Weems, he thought he was gone, or going out of, favour.

'Touched a nerve, eh?' Weems was a man who knew all there was to know about touched nerves and he grinned accordingly. 'Why don't you two get whatever it is sorted? Hah, perhaps it would give us all some satisfaction.'

'The only thing that's likely to get sorted around here, is you, Soddy, if you don't shut that big putrid maw of yours,' Grace warned sternly. Then she called to her barman. 'Lew, give him a free shot, but see he drinks it down the bar. If he makes a sound after that, take him out back and push him head first into a trash can.'

'That's fine, Grace. But it's more'n likely your busthead whiskey is what gave me this big putrid maw in the first place,' Weems said in a drunken, sickly slur.

Will appreciated that Grace's contrived wrangling was an attempt to stop him and Rufus Stone

101

having a serious clash. He glanced past Weems to see Stone's take, but the sheriff's attention was held by something else in the room. By the light from an overhead glass lantern, a living ghost of a man in a faded linen duster was seated alone at a table. He was giving the lawman look-for-look across the smoky haze, and Will cursed silently.

Half out of his mind on a combination of whiskey and quinine sulphate, Sourdough Weems continued to shout abusively.

On Grace Chard's say-so, the barman walked quickly back along the bar. He was making a grab for the drunken liveryman when out of the corner of his eye he saw Rufus Stone suddenly step back, levering a round into the breech of his big Spencer carbine.

It was almost in the same moment that the stranger by the piano grunted for action, throwing his biscuit aside and in one smooth movement bringing up a Colt.

Stone's gun went off with a cannon-like blast in the confines of the saloon. The gunman gasped and his legs buckled. His head dropped and he managed one sideways step as guns suddenly opened fire from every angle. The Chuckwalla filled with uproar, yelling and wild panic as burnt gunpowder filled the air.

A second gunman went crashing to the ground as the man by the piano slammed across the keyboard. There was a discordant clash of sound and he pivoted, rolled slowly to the floor, leaving the keys smeared in crimson.

Inches from Grace's head, a bullet smashed into the long shelf behind her. She gasped, recoiling as bottles and glasses fell to shatter on the floor around her feet. Impulsively, Will vaulted the bar, dragging her down as a bullet snatched a bite from the crown of his hat.

Across the saloon, people were hitting the floor as the sheriff triggered off another two shots. But then he was hit. It was a crease high in the shoulder, hurling him off balance, his carbine pounding a round into one of the hanging lamps, as he stumbled to one knee.

With glass and oil showering down, the saloon was plunged into half-darkness. Will rose from behind the bar, but there were no targets, only confusion and distressed shouting. Grace was calling the sheriff's name, then another voice from the direction of the batwings was hollering for his men to get out and hit leather.

Will didn't draw his gun, just cursed as he squinted through the low, curling smoke. He saw scuffling, dashing figures, listened to the running steps out and along the boardwalk.

'Everyone stay where they are. If anyone o' you tries to leave this place, I'll blast 'em to a goddamn netherworld, so help me.' Stone was angry, but his voice was spiked with authority.

'Whoever those men were, they must have brought their families with 'em,' Grace whispered hoarsely.

'Yeah, the hounds of hell,' Will said, helping her to her feet. 'Are you OK?'

'Living in this town's not for the faint-hearted. I'm fine, thank you, Will.'

'Well, *I'm not*,' a voice crackled from the opposite end of the bar. 'I've spilled me liquor. Good job I didn't pay for it.'

'Looks like you've had some other sort o' accident, Soddy,' somebody jeered at Sourdough Weems's predicament.

But there was a lot less to smile about after happy jack lanterns and wall sconces were lit to survey the damage. Among the bodies that littered the floor, there were three wounded and one dead town man with a bullet in the middle of his chest.

Two of the gunmen who had opened up on Sheriff Stone had fought their last gunfight. Along with the man at the piano, an accomplice lay dead on the floor beside him. He'd been almost chopped in half by the .52 carbine.

When the sheriff returned to the saloon, he didn't appear to be suffering greatly, although the left shoulder of his sack coat was torn and soaked with blood. 'They're ridin' east,' he said, casting a perfunctory eye at the corpses now lined up by the batwings. Then he looked at the wide-eyed, worried faces. 'I'm callin' for a posse to run 'em down. Who wants in?'

But no hands went up and not one man stepped forward as a volunteer. The violence that characterized Blue Wells these days was almost exclusively the work of the man with the badge and a cupboard full of guns. As a result, Sheriff Stone was now interested in pursuit, running the gunmen to earth. The townsfolk were for keeping the trouble at arm's length, watching from a safe distance, then reading about it in the *Basin Bugle*.

'I said, I'm lookin' for posse men,' Stone repeated. 'Don't you men know your duty?'

'Them gunnies ain't our business, so's it ain't our duty, Sheriff,' said a man who had been rolling drunk fifteen minutes earlier.

'Yessir. I never seen all that much, but I seen enough to know the whole goddamn bunch of 'em was after *you*,' another added with a gesture of defiance.

'What the hell's it matter who they were after?' Stone demanded furiously.

'It matters to *them*. It's their lives you're wanting to put on the line,' Will said, evenly. Will thought he perceived a slackening of Stone's grip on events, the control of Blue Wells and Hondo Basin. And it was what he wanted, part of his scheme. As far as he was concerned, if Stone had died from a quick bullet in the saloon, it would have been too easy . . . a grave disappointment. Yeah, he thought. *There's a heap of suffering before you head to them faraway hills.*

'Rufus,' Grace appealed, as the lawman glared back at Will. 'Forget about chasing them. You're wounded and they're long gone now.'

'Goddamnit, Grace,' Stone returned. 'You don't think a handful o' gunmen wanted me *wounded*, do you? Hell no, they'll be back to finish off whatever it was they started, or are gettin' paid for.' The lawman's voice dropped as he realized what he was saying: that it *was him* they were after . . . his business.

Now, all eyes flitted between the sheriff and the dead men. And with every passing moment of silence it became that much clearer that no one from the Chuckwalla was prepared to ride with Stone.

'Then I'll bring 'em in alone,' Stone said, turning back for the door.

'No, Rufus,' Grace cried out in genuine distress. 'Can't somebody stop him? Will?'

'Let him go,' Will advised, taking her by the arm. You don't want to deprive a man of his livelihood, do you? It's what he does, and he knows what he's up against.'

'What are you talking about? There was a gang of them. They'll kill him.'

'Yeah, maybe. Have you thought that those men might have had a reason for doing what they did, Grace? Well, I'll wager your good sheriff has.' Will knew he was touching on the truth, but wasn't sure that Grace was with him. 'The Lord's not the only one who thinks that vengeance is theirs, you know.'

Grace was about to say something, but instead she pulled away, looking at Will as though what she'd just heard was making her afraid.

13

They buried the towner in the high part of the cemetery, the outlaws among the stunt pine and jimson. The plain pine markings for both Ike and Malachi Bound carried the simple carved legend of, 'Unknown Outlaw', and the year of death. It was an educated guess that both men were outlaws because of their murderous intentions in the Chuckwalla saloon. Nobody knew for sure.

Stone had combed through his files in search for details of a likely-sounding pair, but without success. But by their appearance, he was of the opinion that he was dealing with a bunch of desperados from the nameless gulches and canyons of the Sacramentos. He had their descriptions circulated in the hope that one of the law enforcement agencies of the bordering territories might come up with something he could tag a name to.

With his left arm in a makeshift sling, Stone spent many hours with his deputy, hunting for signs, checking out known outlaw haunts. But it was to little avail, and he wasn't for neglecting his town. Most nights he was to be seen, stern-faced, with his big Spencer, walking the main street and its shadowed alleys. The citizens of Blue Wells retired to their beds, safe in the knowledge that their sheriff wasn't too far away. However, there were now some who were wondering about a next time.

Next morning, Will paused on the mercantile's porch to watch Stone and Eben Gent ride out on yet another exploration. The deputy nodded, but Stone didn't even glance his way.

You've seen me, though, Will thought, offering a skew-jawed smile. The sheriff was no fool. He didn't know about Will's intent, or why he was hostile towards him. But he knew they'd never make blood brothers, and regarded him accordingly.

April Winney was her usual severely groomed and attired self. She and Will saw one another frequently, but their relationship seemed to have reached a kind of stalemate. Will knew she was no fool, and that he wasn't just somebody who happened by. It was the secrets he carried that created a stumbling block for their feelings. Once upon a time, he'd have given much, but that was long ago, and now he'd settle for friendship.

'It's a fine morning, Will.'

'And still early,' Will replied with a droll smile, placing a well-worn copy of *The Last of the Mohicans* on the counter. He did most of his reading late at night when sleep eluded him. With the night winds sweeping away the remains of the day, it often seemed to Will that he and Stone were probably the only ones awake in Blue Wells.

April gave him a serious look. 'The sheriff just rode by. He doesn't give up easy, does he?' she said.

'Nope. He'll keep at it until he kills them or they kill him.'

'You sound as if you don't care one way or another.'

'Oh I care, April. I really do,' Will said earnestly, but while running an eye over the shelves behind her. 'What's today's special offer?'

'I have earmarked something for you. *Moby Dick.* You might find it of interest.'

'I've read it, April. Are you thinking I'm a Captain Ahab . . . the whale . . . the boy who survived?'

Within the range of classical adventure stories,

Will's reading was extensive. He had spent time in a place where – other than breaking rocks – men had little more to do than think or sleep sixteen hours out of every twenty-four.

A moment later, April brought him a copy of *The Song of Hiawatha*. 'I'll be surprised if you've read *this*,' she suggested. They stood chatting about books and stories in general until Will glanced at the clock above the counter.

'I'm meeting Hector Speke out at Carlo's Jug in fifteen minutes,' he said.

'You've time. I wish you'd drop that case against the sheriff, Will,' she replied, a little sharper than she'd meant.

'It's not *my* case.'

'Everybody knows Speke hasn't got the bristle or resources to go ahead without support. He hasn't got two cents to rub together.'

'That doesn't mean the case is any less his. I hope you're not one of those who consider the sheriff to be above the law. The law he's paid to uphold?' he added with a penetrating smile.

'No, I'm not one of those, Will. I consider Sheriff Stone to be a peace officer of some integrity. Sometimes a tad high-handed, but—'

'But he's a servant, nevertheless,' Will interrupted. 'Maybe that Speke case will serve him as a reminder.'

April looked left and right to make certain nobody could overhear before she spoke again. 'Do you trust me, Will?' she asked.

'Ma'am, you look the most trusting person I ever did see. Why'd you ask?'

'Would you say we were friends?' she continued.

'Yes, ma'am. You look just about the friendliest friend I ever did have.'

'Stop kidding me, Will Jarrow. I want to know what's between you and Sheriff Stone. No one else is ever going to ask. They're too frightened.'

For the shortest moment, Will felt the temptation to tell her. But he resisted it. He'd tell her when the time came, after he'd done what he had to do, not before.

'That's their problem. But what's it to you, April?' he parried.

'I don't want to see another dreadful, useless tragedy played out in the street. I'd rather not be here.'

'You don't want to see anything happen to your esteemed sheriff. Is that what you mean?'

'No. I mean you, you knucklehead. Now go before you're late for that meeting.'

Will felt unnerved as he picked up his book. He could see that April meant what she said, but it had been a long time since anyone gave a damn about whether he lived or died.

'I can take care of me,' he said brusquely. 'If it's advice you're handing out, go give some to Stone. Unless of course you don't think he'd listen.'

His hurtful words hit home. But in a strange way, he meant them to, and it didn't bother him too much. Whatever feelings Will had for April Winney, they were small peas compared to the bleak emotions he held for Rufus Stone.

Pigeons stood dopey with sleep on the rooftops along the main street. A bent-legged dog followed at a distance as Will walked towards the centre of town. It was a warm day, and Blue Wells seemed to be slumbering contentedly under the bright sunshine. He passed the Chuckwalla where carpenters and glaziers had made good the splintered traces of the gun battle, then on by the undertakers where trade had dwindled. Shutters were drawn at the jailhouse, locked safe and secure during the lawmen's absence. It was only a minute or two past ten when he strolled into Carlo's Jug, but Hector Speke wasn't there, just his note.

'He ain't here, Mr Jarrow. He left this note, though,' Carlo informed him.

'Thank you. When did you see him?'

'Daybreak, this mornin'.'

Will stared at the letter. He didn't really have to read it. He had a good idea about the content. Hector Speke had been very twitchy since the recent gunfight at the Chuckwalla. He'd seen men die, and Rufus Stone establish himself yet again as the most formidable, resilient man in Hondo Basin.

Will guessed that Speke would catch a big dose of fear, and he was right. The pitiable land breaker was apologetic in his note, sorry that he couldn't go through with the lawsuit. He was off to Tombstone to try his luck at the silver diggings, and then for the California gold. He closed with the suggestion that Will might be well advised to follow suit. 'You never said what it was you had against the sheriff', he wrote. 'But whatever it is, he'll shoot you down. I'm getting out before he shoots us both.'

When a glass and bottle banged down in front of him, Will folded the letter away.

'My finest French brandy,' Carlo said and grinned. 'He quit, did he, your friend Speke?'

Will poured himself a few fingers of raw corn, drinking it in one long pull. 'Yeah. Big surprise.'

'You mean smart. It's his own way of gettin' to live longer.'

114

'Do something for me, will you, Carlo? Just for a while. Keep your opinions to yourself, and your mouth shut.'

Will ripped the note in half, crumpled the pieces in his fist and dropped them on the sopping counter. 'Useful for the privy,' he said and left the bar.

Making his way back into town, he stopped off at Attorney Daggert's to discuss the possibility of proceeding against the sheriff without the chief witness, but the attorney turned him down, said he'd wasted enough money already.

'How's your luck, feller?' Oleg Halstrom called out a few minutes later. He was standing in the doorway of the newspaper office watching the street, hopeful for something local to report.

Will made a remark about luck not being something to trust, but Halstrom continued. 'Can you spare me a moment or two?'

Inside the office, Halstrom beckoned for Will to take a seat while he sat against the front of his desk. 'Do you recall that talk we had about the sheriff's daughter?' he asked.

'Yeah, I remember what you said. I remember most stuff. So what?'

'I did some checking through a friend of mine who works on the Santa Rosa Dispatch. Santa

Rosa's where Stone wore the badge before coming here. But you knew that, didn't you?'

'Are you asking or telling?'

'Confirming. Well, I asked this friend if there was more to the story about that girl's death than was revealed. He told me there was. So, all that you had to say about Stone's daughter running off to meet someone is true. Apparently, some did get hold of the story but agreed to hush it up when Stone asked them to.'

'Yeah, that's more or less what happened. But I told you that,' Will pointed out.

'You did, yes. But there was an important part you left out. My informant says there was a rumour that the sheriff's daughter was eloping with some no-good outlaw. That was why Stone did what he did, to try and stop her. There's always another side, don't you think?'

Will gave him a steely glare before answering. 'Stone found all that out *after* Natalie died. He tried to stop her because he was a son-of-a-bitch who wouldn't have his own flesh and blood put his goddamn doctrine to the test. *He* was responsible for the death of his own daughter. Why don't you give that story some column inches? It's the truth.'

'*Natalie, eh?* Who was it she was going to meet that night, Will?'

116

But Will didn't reply. He got up from the chair, without another word, and stepped back onto the street. He walked past people without seeing them, remote, returning again to the desolate feelings and thoughts that haunted him.

Will was alone in a railcar as it clicked and clacked its way through the lethal night storm towards El Paso. But he wasn't going to be alone for long. Natalie was going to join him at the mainline station. She didn't care that he was on the dodge from the law. She believed him when he said that the charge of bank robbery against him was one of mistaken identity. From the moment they'd first met on the streets of Portales during her short break from Santa Rosa, she had believed everything he told her. It was nothing but the truth. He was innocent. When the law caught up with him, he sent her back home, while he fled to somewhere west of the Carlsbad Caverns. Eventually, he wired her asking her to meet him at El Paso. They would journey west to Arizona, then on to California for a new life.

The pursuing lawmen knew he was likely going to run west, what route he'd be taking. But the telegraph was temporarily down along the southern stretch, and if they kept travelling, they weren't going to be overtaken and caught. It was a lot to ask, for Natalie to share a life on the owl hoot. But Will knew that in time he would acquit himself, and there was no other way for them to be together.

In El Paso, the rain was torrential, shrouding station lamps, diffusing light from the windows of the train carriages. A conductor in gleaming oil-skins was waving the last of the passengers aboard as Will ran from end to end of the westbound platform, desperately searching for the familiar face. A final whistle pierced the wildness, and Will had to make up his mind whether to stay and risk arrest, or to climb aboard, accept that something terrible must have happened to prevent Natalie coming to meet him.

So he went alone, travelling west and crushed from the torment of not knowing what had happened. He disembarked and went into hiding at Lordsburg, sending wires almost daily back to Santa Rosa. Then he read the news, the story of Sheriff Stone's daughter who'd died from pneumonia. The following day he received a letter from Natalie's friend. She'd told the gut-wrenching facts of how the woman he'd fallen in love with had died soon after that fateful, storm-lashed night.

Hounded by lawmen once again, Will continued

his way across Arizona towards the California border. But now he was disillusioned and heedless. Eventually he was caught, and at a summary trial convicted and sent to Yuma Penitentiary to break ground for the Gila Turnpike.

Determined to prove his innocence and free himself from where the over-zealous law had thrown him, Will read as many law books as he could lay his hands on. After two years – and more by blessed chance than intent – a drifting horse-wrangler confessed to the crime for which Will had been found guilty. But all the learning paid off. It enabled Will to strike home his case for repara-tion, provide him with the resources he needed to square an account for the death of Natalie.

And now in the town of Blue Wells, that man was under his nose, still waiting and wanting to kill. Rufus Stone, a once respectable lawman, now turned outlaw killer. An obsessed sheriff who would shoot men down for the rest of his days in the despairing hope that one of them would be the man he held responsible for the death of his daughter.

'Cheer up, Mr Jarrow, it might never happen,' someone called out from the street.

The voice brought Will up from his dark reverie

of a girl stumbling her way through a violent night, frantically needing to reach a westbound train.

'It already has,' he returned icily, stopping for a moment to get his bearings. 'I'm just going up to see there's an available plot.'

From talking to Halstrom at the newspaper office, Will was just past Carlo's Jug, cemetery side of the tannery. He breathed deep, clenched his fists. All of a sudden, it wasn't enough to see Stone's body roped to a photographer's plank. It was a warranted ending maybe, poetic even, but not enough. How pitiless he was going to be filled his head with new thoughts.

14

Deputy Eben Gent calmly rode the old prospec-
tors' trail which wound down from the hills south
of Hondo Basin. He was heading back to Blue
Wells following another unsuccessful day's search
in the company of the sheriff. He had wanted to
check out a couple of grub shacks before calling it
quits. Stone had agreed, returning before dusk,
wanting to be on hand when the usual Saturday
night roostering began.

Gent was now riding alone under a clear, star-
studded sky, when the mounted figures appeared
without warning on the trail ahead. In an instant,
the deputy sawed at the reins, dug spurs and
pulled his Colt. He didn't have time to wonder if
Stone would have been proud of him, the way he
took action before the guns ahead of him crashed

121

out, ripping great yellow gashes in the darkness.

Violent hammer blows of pain caught the young deputy's body as he frantically wheeled his mount. He felt bullets strike his horse, heard them whine off a trailside rock. He gave a futile jab, then a rake with his spurs as the horse's front legs buckled. He hit the ground hard, rolling and skidding in the shale and weeds. For the shortest moment, and with his face stinging from rock-nettle and acrid dirt, he heard dull footsteps, then more bullets thudded into the middle of his back.

Eels Painter sipped and swallowed, then stared at the grimy glass. He hardly ate any more, was under no illusions that raw liquor was all that was keeping him going. 'A rattler would be proud to spit some o' the stuff I have,' he choked out with bitter laughter. He could still sit in a saddle, but it was a sadistic task. It had taken days to recover from the headlong flight from Blue Wells – the night Ike and Malachi Bound fell to Rufus Stone's big Spencer carbine.

Yet sick and wasted as he was, Painter was in an upbeat mood, indicating that Ed McNiece and John Kress continue with their reports.

'Yeah, was like shootin' fish in a barrel,' said the darkly featured McNiece.

122

'Easier,' grinned Kress, the candy-chewing gunman. He tossed something onto the table where Painter was sitting. 'Little trophy, Boss,' he said.

Painter didn't touch the bloodied deputy sheriff's badge. He somehow knew it wouldn't be the sheriff's star. Lawmen of Rufus Stone's calibre didn't fall that easy.

'You done real good, boys,' he wheezed. From his base in the decrepit log cabin in the hills, Painter had kept his three men in the saddle, having them watch the search patterns of the Blue Wells sheriffs. There were few better at that sort of furtive surveillance than the riders from the rugged Sacramentos. They reported in on the lawmens' movements each night, and Painter bided his time. When Stone rode back to Blue Wells, it was the mistake he'd been waiting for, and he sent McNiece and Kress out to do their work.

'Well, he's on his own now, Boss,' Rex Ferry said.

'Yeah, *all alone*,' Painter confirmed, gazing pensively around him. 'Makes it one against four.'

'Them's my kind of odds,' Ferry grinned and started to giggle. 'I'm always up for a fair fight.'

But Kress wasn't amused. 'It was one against *six* at the Chuckwalla. You forgotten that?' he rasped.

Coughing, Painter got up and moved about the

cabin to encourage some life into his bones. 'There was a lot wrong that night,' he said. 'I wanted Stone, an' I wanted him to know where it was comin' from. I just never reckoned on him bein' such a goddamn, hard-boiled son-of-a-bitch.'

'Well, he's *still* a goddamn, hard-boiled son-of-a-bitch. We'll take him a different way,' Rex Ferry proposed. The man made up in recklessness what he lacked in any gun skill or brains. 'Let's get him planked and stood in the place he put Laguna. What do you say, Boss?'

'I welcome your sentiments, Rex. But I ain't hankerin' to lose any more good men,' Painter vowed. The old man didn't want to go back into the Sacramentos alone. And he didn't want to be alone when grit and strong liquor gave out to the contagion in his lungs. 'I figure he'll stick to town limits when he finds out his deputy's gone,' he said. 'He ain't afraid, but he'll be as nervy as a wring-tail after this. He won't make another mistake.'

'How about a weakness?' Ferry asked.

'A weakness? You know of one?'

'Yeah. The eye-catchin' saloon lady. There was somethin' between 'em. I reckon he'll be on a regular visit.'

Painter wiped the back of his hand across his

mouth. 'I wasn't plannin' to go back to that place,' he remarked. 'We wouldn't be right welcome.'

'How about that place just out o' the town?' suggested McNiece. 'I seen him poke his nose in there the night o' the shoot-out. It's dark an' unfriendly, an' if we can't catch an' drop him there, we're all of us in the wrong line o' work.'

'Yeah, Carlo's Jug,' Kress agreed, smacking the flap of his pouch holster. 'It's full o' swillpots, Boss. Not much chance of anyone bein' interested in our business. That's the point o' them sort o' places.'

Painter considered for a moment. He would have taken a bit more time to devise a plan, had he felt he had any time left. But he was a man on a short rope. 'Okay,' he decided, a cough reminding him again of his alternative fight. 'We'll ride in tomorrow night. It sounds like asses on plush compared to this dump.'

'Are you sure you're up to it, Eels?' Kress asked.

'Yeah, you don't *have* to be there,' McNiece added.

'Yes I do.' Painter's voice was hard-edged. He was burnt out, empty as a war drum with only rocks of hatred cracking around inside. But it was enough. All he wanted was to witness the finish of the lawman who'd killed his son. He wiped his mouth again. 'I'll last that long,' he promised.

Kress still had some concern. 'Did any o' you remember seein' a tall feller standing at the end o' the bar in the Chuckwalla?' he asked thoughtfully.

'What about him?' McNiece asked.

'I dunno. There was somethin' about him, though. He didn't panic, but didn't get involved either. I saw him standin' there watchin' when we scarpered, an' wondered if they were workin' together.'

'I was told about a joker who shouted to Stone when Laguna was fixin' to gun him,' Ferry said. 'Perhaps it's him.'

Painter scowled. 'I never knew about any o' that.' He clenched a tight, bony fist and the brows tightened over his eyes again. 'Don't matter. If there is some sort of amity, we'll take 'em both.'

So it was decided. As Painter started coughing again, his men took their leave, went out to tend the horses before settling in for the night. Nowadays, Eels Painter felt the cold cruelly, and he brushed the toe of his boot through the fire's embers. He threw on some more tinder and another log, standing close and staring into the low flames. *There was a time I had some o' life's juices to get warm,* he thought bleakly.

15

Going to take a look at the body of Eben Gent had been a mistake, Will realized. He met Rufus Stone on the walkway outside of Lincoln's smithy, and they exchanged a cold stare. The sheriff had discarded his sling, and, looking near to his old formidable self, steadily held Will's eyes. If the man had been touched by shock or grief, he wasn't showing it.

'You satisfied now, Jarrow?' he asked.

'Satisfied? What the hell are you talking about?'

'One of us down an' one to go. Ain't that your interest in this town?'

'I still don't know what the hell you're talking about, Stone. I don't figure in this, and you know it,' Will answered sharply. 'From what I heard, the death of that deputy is down to you. Like so many

127

other young bloods,' he added with bite.

For a deep moment, Stone thought on Will's words. 'Yeah, I think I'm gettin' it,' he said. 'You came to town for a funeral that ain't happened yet. But I'll tell you this,' he added, lifting the barrel of his carbine for added authority. 'Sooner or later I'll find out if I'm right, an' if you're still around, I'll bring you down for it. That's a promise.'

'Something to live for, eh?' Will replied. 'Tell me, Sheriff Stone, you ever seen a dog rub itself into carrion? It's the stench o' death they love . . . the way it sticks to 'em.'

'Be real careful, Jarrow. Watchful too. Make one small mistake from now on, an' I'll close that smart mouth o' yours for good.'

'Yeah, I will. Just you remember that from now on I won't be the one who gives you warning.' Will gave a sharp double woof as he walked away. When he stopped on the next corner to glance back, the sheriff had gone.

For the next few minutes, Will tried to concentrate on the present. Despite what he had just told the sheriff, there seemed little doubt that the Painter gang had been responsible for the death of Eben Gent. And that meant they hadn't fled Hondo Basin as most people suspected. They were obviously still around, and, whatever their motive, likely wanted to finish the job they'd bloodily botched at the Chuckwalla.

Why sick old Eels Painter and his guns were after Rufus Stone didn't interest Will that much. What concerned him was if they should kill Stone before he had the chance. An opportune moment had just presented itself when he could have provoked the man into a fight.

With that notion in mind, the question suddenly occurred to Will as to whether or not Stone dying at the hands of someone else would be so bad. *Goddamnit, I've been here too long*, he thought. *I've got to know the man. Time and familiarity's dulled the edge.* And seeing the deputy's bullet-riddled body hadn't helped him. The sight of another young lifeless face had chiggered in. Right now, Will doubted if an eye for an eye was what he really wanted.

Well done, Will, he thought. A big slice of my life wasted. And then, *No, must be a passing weakness. It'll come back.* He knew at that moment it was time for him to ride out. He should take his buckskin for a run, find some wind to blow doubt and confusion from his mind.

It was Oleg Halstrom who called out, when he was almost at the livery. 'Hey, feller, slow down, will you? I was always told to beware the hurry-up man.'

'It sounds like smart advice. What is it this time?'

Will's manner was instantly brusque. He had avoided the newsman since their last conversation when he'd allowed himself to reveal too much.

'Bad business about Deputy Gent,' Halstrom said.

'Yeah, but it sort of goes with the territory. When you catch up with the outlaws you're hunting, they hardly ever invite you to join 'em for coffee,' Will replied with a callousness he didn't feel.

'I guess they killed him on account they didn't have the guts to go for the sheriff?'

'Well, he wasn't there, was he? You can take that any way you want. Is that it?'

'Not quite. I saw you talking to Stone back there,' Halstrom continued. 'He's got the notion in his head that you know something. As he himself put it, "somethin' stuck in your craw". It got me to thinking that I'm a tad further down the line than him on that one.'

Will gave an inscrutable look, but he wanted to know if there was anything else on Halstrom's mind. 'You want me to agree with you?'

'Not on that, no. I asked you something a while back, and you didn't answer because you didn't have to. It was you on the train that night, wasn't it? You were the outlaw Natalie Stone was going to meet in El Paso.'

This time, Will offered a tight smile and a shake of his head. 'Shame there's no mention of that in the *Bugle*. Then we'd all know it was fiction.'

'I don't think so. It all ties in. What you're doing in Blue Wells. The way you've been shadowing the sheriff. The detail about his daughter's death. Yeah, it was you she was eloping with . . . the night her pa locked her in the house. You're here to avenge her.'

'Aren't you forgetting it was me who saved his life when the Mex tried to kill him?'

'That makes some sort of sense, too. The taking of his life is what *you* wanted . . . the dubious pleasure. I'm right, aren't I?'

'You think I'd tell you, if you were?'

'Hate's like cancer, Will. It eats you up . . . gives a lot of pain before it sure as hell kills you.' Halstrom grabbed Will's arm. 'Just listen to what I'm saying. If I have to go to Stone with what I suspect about you and your purpose, I will. You can see that, can't you?'

'Yeah. But you won't.'

'Why not?'

'Because the man's a killer. You and your smug towner folk might go around with all that jawbone about him being the law and justice and keeping you safe. But deep down you know he's as much a

131

killer as them who gunned down the deputy. Stone just wears a badge while he's doing it. You won't tell him what you reckon you know, because then he'll try and kill me. Now you tell me that *I'm* right.'

Halstrom's shoulders dropped in defeat. He'd been got the better of and they both knew it. 'It's not going to take him much longer to work out who you are,' he said. 'You could leave town. Do us all a favour.'

'It's been too long for me to do that,' Will retorted and walked away.

Halstrom returned to his office. Caught between the stools of newspaper editor and law-abiding citizen, he was wondering if anything had changed, what it was he had to inform the sheriff about.

Sourdough Weems was sitting in a wedge of sunlight outside of the livery. He was soaping up a heavy Denver saddle when Will turned up. He paused in his work, squinting as he reached for a bottle.

'Head's ringin' like a cook's angle iron,' he said histrionically.

'One day someone's going to come in here and shoot your goddamn jaw off. That'll shut you up, you miserable wretch. I'm taking the buckskin out for some fresh air,' he rasped and went inside.

Weems unstoppered a quart of trade whiskey, almost falling from the bench as the fumes hit. Never really knowing when something he swallowed might poison him beyond recovery, he took a long pull, rinsed it around his mouth and rolled his bloodshot eyes.

'Hah. Why don't you take Miss April for a buggy ride?' he called out, punching the cork back into the jar. 'Who the hell wants to go off on their own like some sad ol' lobo? Drive her into the moonlight. But do it before the month's out 'cause we got a goose drownder comin'. I can smell it.'

A few moments later, Will appeared in the doorway. 'I don't need your smart-ass advice on what to do,' he scowled.

Weems shrugged and spat on the leather. 'It ain't advice. I was just sayin'.'

'Sorry, Sourdough. Perhaps you're not always such a miserable old harpy. Buggy ride, you say?'

'Yeah. Miss April was tellin' my missus that you mentioned it to her last weekend. Apparently, she was real disappointed you never got around to it.'

Will stared off towards the distant timberline. He was only going to brood on things if he went out there alone. He didn't know the rights and wrongs of it, whether he was just using April Winney, but right now, a few hours in her diverting company wouldn't harm.

He glanced at Weems, who was smirking. 'Unsaddle my horse,' he said. 'I've got to go see someone about a book.'

16

'Good evening, Sheriff. Have you come to say you're eating with me, or that you're favouring a patrol of the town?'

'The latter, I'm afraid, Grace, and it's nothing to do with favouring,' Stone replied with a hollow smile.

'You do look bushed, Rufus. I can see it in your face, your eyes. Surely just for once. . . ?'

'It'll be that once . . . the first time, when someone's waiting for me, the soft option.'

'That's paranoia, Rufus. Eben's death has got to you. We could have supper in my rooms, and you could watch your precious town from the window if it's that important. Take a late watch.'

'It's tempting, Grace. Mighty tempting. But duty's duty.'

'Yes, like pig-headed's pig-headed, and before pleasure. Always before pleasure.'

'Huh, you'll be serving flat beer and weak whiskey next, Grace. No, I won't risk somebody being harmed or robbed because of my disregard for what's right. You wouldn't want it any different.'

Grace forced a little smile in return. 'I wonder if I should give it a try. Being upright can be mighty tiring, Rufus. If you're back before the night's through, we'll share a canned special.'

'What's that?'

'Peaches and sweet milk.'

'I'll be back,' Stone assured her, touching his hat brim in acknowledgement.

There was a groundswell of public opinion against Stone's brutal implementation as peace officer, but he was greeted with reserved respect as he left the Chuckwalla. Tonight, the good folk of Blue Wells were all with him. The town was jittery, and he was riding on the back of Eben Gent being a popular citizen as well as a deputy sheriff.

A buck board wheeled past as he paused on the edge of the saloon's porch. The man and woman on the spring seat had their collars turned up against the evening chill, but before they swung west towards the foothill trail, he recognized April

Winney and Will Jarrow.

He checked his big Spencer, and his .36 belly gun, before stepping down and taking the centre of the street. *I won't give you an easy shot*, he thought, his eyes raking shadows and alleyways. *Whoever you are, I'll make you goddamn aim.* It was a cold, clear night, and the big moon threw his dark shadow ahead of him. He didn't make a detour or cut any corners as he strode watchfully to the north end of town, his mind working overtime on possibilities and outcomes.

He bitterly regretted that he'd never caught up with Eels Painter and his gang, but knew it was only a matter of time, sooner more than later. The remaining outlaws were obviously prowling the valley, waiting for their chance at him, and he felt culpable about Eben Gent stopping bullets that were undoubtedly meant for him. But with each wanted man who got planked and added to his rogues gallery, his burden of resentment was eased a little. *Somewhere out there, there's a bullet with my name on it. Who the hell are you an' when do we meet?* he wondered, cursing and shuddering at the myriad thoughts.

He halted by a long hitch rail outside of the tannery, turning to stare back along the main street, then west across the moonlit rangeland. He wanted to be out there hunting down killers, but that would be unprofessional and reckless. He was a fair tracker and a good gunhand, yet the prospect of hunting a pack of outlaws in the wilds was foolishly risky. He had sent a wire to Greenfield for assistance, but until they responded, he would keep within town limits.

He returned to musing on the old, wraithlike Painter, and who he likely was; guessing rightly that the man was blood to somebody he'd killed and that he'd come again. I can feel you watching me, goddamnit, he thought. *Well, you won't be coming mob-handed again, that's for sure. And my bullets come cheaper by the boxload.* Stone held enough grit and determination to take on each and every outlaw who felt up to it. He welcomed them, living each and every day with the prospect that one day he'd bring down the one that mattered. The man who'd lured his daughter Natalie away from Santa Rosa that fateful night.

Beyond the ditch that oozed with effluent from the tannery, the lights of Carlo's Jug glowed weak and yellow. A drunk staggered diagonally across the road, tottering, nearly falling as Stone approached.

'Get yourself home, Rourke,' Stone said, not unkindly. 'If you fall in this mess, no one's going to rescue you. And you won't be spending the night in one o' my cells.'

The prone figure saluted the sky. 'Yessir, Sheriff. I'll just take me a bearin'.'

Stone waited until the drunk got up and headed towards the town, then he stepped onto the low decking outside of the false-fronted structure, listening for a moment before entering.

The drinking place was quiet, but there did appear to be a few more than the usual number of patrons. There were the regular stiffs and swillpots, some of them sharing the luxury of a table with a candle lamp. Back against the canvas walls where the shadows were deeper, figures sat with hat brims pulled low across their faces. *I'll get me some town ordinance that prohibits that sort of thing,* was Stone's first thought. *Best place to sleep off a soak, I suppose,* was his second, wry observation. The air was rank with stale body sweat and tobacco smoke, stagnant fumes from the skin and hide works. But he cursed under his breath, because there was something stirring another sense.

He scanned the room again, and this time he caught sight of a movement to the side of and just beyond the timber bar. One of two canvas screen flaps had been pulled aside and the deathly-looking face of Eels Painter was staring out at him.

Cold sweat broke between his shoulder blades, and he shivered. Then he cursed again, had the shortest moment to react before the first gun thundered out.

He threw himself to the ground, squirming beneath a nearby table as the room erupted with an amazing storm of sound. *They knew where I'd be,* he seethed as lead ploughed into the tables and chairs, puckering the hard-packed dirt floor around him. Bullets tore through the makeshift saloon's canvas walls, and two crocks of Taos Aguardiente were shattered. *They're trying to get me with blanket firepower,* he realised. *Two, three, maybe four of them.*

Stepping away from the cover of the other hanging flap of canvas, John Kress held his Colt in a two-handed grip. He fired levelly, and his aim was good. His target threw up an arm, grunted in pain and crumpled to the ground.

'That ain't him,' Ed McNiece snarled out. 'That ain't Stone.'

'No, this is, and I know where you are,' Stone yelled back in reply.

The darkly featured McNiece was lifted off his feet, flung backwards as a .52 calibre bullet hammered into his body. Stone fired again, then rolled violently away from the table as Kress, Painter and

Rex Ferry cut loose with another lethal fusillade.

But now the adrenalin had kicked in, and Stone's verve returned. Lying on his side, he wrenched another shell into the carbine's chamber, then rolled back to the pulverized table. He placed the carbine on the ground beside him, drew his belly gun and got to his feet. 'It ain't God's work but it's what I do best,' he shouted, putting two bullets into the copper-headed Rex Ferry.

The youngster's throat broke apart in a crimson pulp. His knees buckled and he toppled sideways, pitifully clutching the long duster of Eels Painter as he fell.

Stone's next bullet demolished a lamp on the end of the bar. As hot oil and flames spilled out along the counter top, the old man fired back almost indiscriminately. 'Damn him to hell,' he howled.

'We should never have come back,' Kress gasped, holding his side where he'd been hit. 'The man's homicidal. Let's clear this place for good.'

A blast from Stone's carbine almost severed a central strut, sending both men running for the rear of the saloon and a way out. Filled with anger and frustration, and despite the menace of the big Spencer, Kress turned. He gave reckless covering

141

fire until he saw the sheriff throw himself into cover once again.

'Kill him. Finish him off.' Painter's voice was no more than a desperate squeal to his top gunman.

But Kress was in pain, and he'd had enough. 'He won't die, goddamnit,' he yelled. 'But we will, unless we get out o' here.'

Stone was more stunned than hurt, sprawled on the floor with a dark bloodstain soaking the top of his left arm. 'Come out of this alive, Rufus, and I might consider retiring,' he rasped.

The sheriff was a sitting duck for anyone with enough grit to finish him off. But Kress and Painter had pushed their way out through a back flap in the saloon's canvas walls. They'd fled into the night, and Blue Wells would be burying a second brace from the Painter gang.

17

Will Jarrow pointed his Colt at the snakes that were writhing beneath his feet. *Wanting the higher ground,* he thought. *Trying to escape the flood.* Then he realized they were only shapes his mind was creating in the darkness, and he shuddered, cursing silently. But it was a warning, and it alerted him to the sound of approaching hoofbeats back along the trail.

A mile distant, April Winney was driving the buck board back to town. Will had insisted she leave when he realized that the two riders, who had ridden frantically from Blue Wells in the aftermath of the gunfire, were heading directly towards them. He didn't know who they were or what the next few minutes might bring, but he backed trouble, and didn't want her involved.

Two men rode around a darkly silhouetted dogwood brake, and came straight on towards him. He recognized Eels Painter, immediately, the other man as a paid gunny.

'Whoa there, gents,' he shouted, stepping out from beside the trail. 'In this light I could be destroying your knee or your head. Let's hold up a while.'

But John Kress was in no mood to be restrained. He replied with a gun blast that lit up the night.

It was the mistake that Will had already thought out and he fired twice. Kress grunted, twisted and collapsed from his saddle as Will's Colt swung at Painter. Will cursed with aggravation and fired again. It was a rough shot in the darkness, and Painter's horse squealed as it was hit. It threw its head forward into flight, but its legs buckled, sending it crashing to the ground.

Painter struggled to his feet and tried to attack Will with bare, bony fists.

'What the hell's going on? Who the hell are you?' Will shouted, holding the old man off until a coughing fit forced him to his knees.

'I only wanted to kill him. Why'd the son-of-a-bitch make it so difficult?'

'Who did you want to kill? Who are you talking about?' Will demanded.

144

'Rufus Stone. The sheriff o' Blue Wells.' Painter dragged out the words, before slumping into another pain-filled spasm. When he'd got some breath back, he told Will who he was, what had happened in town and why. 'The secret of who I am's no longer any use to me, or anyone else,' he groaned.

Will listened, patient and fascinated as the old man talked about his dead son, his mission of hate, his own looming death. When he had little else to say, Will was quiet for a few moments, lost in thought. Then he gave Painter an idea. A proposal not so much about revenge, more a last wish, bene-faction for a sick man whose feelings for Rufus Stone were as intense as his own.

A few hours ahead of an impending storm, and in response to the wire that Rufus Stone had sent for assistance, a US Marshal arrived at first dark the following day. Because of the high death toll from the gunfight at Carlo's Jug, and the annihilation of the Painter gang, no one carried any objection. Most citizens thought it about time that a territor-ial and unprejudiced lawman should assist Blue Wells in getting get back to some sort of stability.

Even the most ardent Stone supporters, although greatly impressed by the sheriff's stand against the outlaws, were a little jaundiced by the continual death toll. 'When's this killing going to end?' was an increasingly heard question. 'Ain't the way to bring in business,' someone grumbled. 'Not unless you're a boxmaker, or a gravedigger,' someone else added.

Marshal Warren Chimes, a man of severe appearance and temperament, agreed. He said he didn't want to waste his own time or anyone else's, and called for a meeting to be held at noon the following day.

'There's some big water following me, and it's got a warrant to clean this town up, if we don't get it done tomorrow,' he warned, assisted by a venerable smile.

18

The storm arrived at midnight, and within a few hours the town's main street was a sea of mud. The rain drummed unceasingly on the roofs of the buildings. It ran down the clapboards and canvas walls, flooded yards and alleyways, and store windows looked like sheets of water. Then the wind took a hand, sweeping in from the Sacramentos and the rugged hills west and north of the town. It became difficult for even the hardiest souls to negotiate the street, treading the glistening timbers that formed the boardwalks, decks that sank beneath the rising mud.

'No one's looking to fault your achievements, Sheriff, least of all me,' Chimes said from the relative comfort of the improvised meeting house. 'Huh, you don't get to where we are by blowing

147

kisses.' He tapped a list on the bench before him. 'It's just that this is more like a body count from Chickamauga. A hard one to defend, Rufus.'

Some heads nodded, some shook, and Will Jarrow realized why a US Marshal had come to town. The state bigwigs weren't as fully aware of what had been going on as many Blue Wells folk seemed to think. They knew that Rufus Stone held the pennant of law fearlessly high, but for reasons best known to themselves, remained indifferent to the bloody cost.

The mayor spoke up in the sheriff's defence, albeit a tad half-hearted. He was likewise supported by the bank manager and several other agents and merchants. Rufus Stone sat silent and aloof. With a sling supporting his left arm and shoulder, he showed no regret over the latest eruption of bloodshed, not even a pretence.

Some other time, some other place, Will might have admired the haughty composure if he hadn't felt such loathing. Seated to one side, and watching Stone closely, he was thinking back, reminding himself of the fateful night the man's pitiless temperament had driven Natalie away.

And now, under a similar wild storm, Will was prepared to fulfil his long-held mission. *Yeah,* he thought with an icy smile. *It's right. No more doubts.*

As he watched Stone get to his feet, he knew this time he would see it through to the end.

Sheriff Rufus Stone was puffed up, clearly indignant that any law official from Greenfield should be audacious enough to show disapproval, even question his methods. Stone believed the West would be a better place if all peace officers employed his ruthless tactics against miscreants and lawbreakers. Times might be changing, but he wasn't, goddamnit.

Not too far away, out in the main street, a man tugged at the brim of his hat before walking from the shelter of an overhang. From where he'd been waiting patiently, he stepped off the boardwalk, watched the muddy water swirl around his boots, as though fascinated by the movement. Then he looked up slowly and started to cross the street. He lost his footing in a deep wheel rut, cursed and went on, stumbling and falling full length in the mire. He dragged himself to his feet and plunged ahead, avoiding floating garbage and a drowned rat, before reaching the far raised walkway. Peering through the deluge, he grasped an upright for a moment, then made his way to Ma Kettle's Mercantile.

From inside the makeshift meeting room, Will's attention turned to the front door as it suddenly swung open. The door was caught by the rain and the wind, whipping back and forth wildly until it was slammed shut by Oleg Halstrom. Then it opened again, and the ghostly apparition of Eels Painter was standing in the doorway.

'Welcome to your memorial service, Stone,' the old man rasped out.

The sheriff's reaction was quicker than anyone else in the room. He saw the man who had twice tried to kill him, loom close and very menacing. Knowing of no other way to respond in such a crisis, he snorted angrily and drew his belly gun. He had fired twice before Painter could return any sort of challenging movement.

Two bullets ripped into the old man's sickly chest. But so slight was his body that he barely seemed to notice the shocking, hammer-like impact. He fell forward with a twisted smile on his mouth, a skeletal hand pointing accusingly at Stone. Then the hand curved downwards and he followed, trying to stifle a cough as he crumpled into the floorboards.

Will cursed, and hurried to Painter's side. He stared at the ooze of bright blood across the front of the soaking duster, cursing again in astonishment when he saw the old man wasn't carrying a gun. 'What the hell are you doing?' he asked, kneeling close. 'This isn't what we agreed.'

Painter looked up at Will, his dying voice hardly audible. 'Sorry, son. I never was much for agreements. Yours was a good idea, but you'd have swung for it. Besides, I'm already dead from rotten lungs,' he added, closing his pale watery eyes.

'Jesus, is that who the hell I think it is?' Warren Chimes gasped.

Stone took an unhurried step closer to the dead man. 'His name's Eels Painter,' he said. 'He must have had real demons in his head to try something crazy like that.'

'But not crazy enough to carry a gun,' Will seethed. 'His son was Laguna Paris. You remember him?'

'So he's another father wanting revenge.'

'How was he supposed to do that, Stone? Thumb his nose?' Will asked, easing himself upright to face the sheriff. 'He was unarmed, you murdering son-of-a-bitch.'

Stone gave a scowl, not fully understanding what Will meant. But it wasn't long before everyone in the room got the full meaning. Not only was there no weapon in either of the dead outlaw's frail hands, but a search failed to locate one anywhere else.

Some of the blood now drained from Stone's

face as he turned to Chimes. 'You all saw the way he stood there. You heard what he said. He sure as hell made out he had a gun.'

'Well, he didn't.' Will was now one of two or three people not clustered around Painter's corpse. 'So let's all see and hear you get out of this,' he charged bitterly.

'Damn you, Jarrow. We can do without your say,' Stone retaliated.

Will looked at Chimes. 'One or two low-down places I've passed through might raise an eyebrow at that killing. If it's confirmation you've come to Blue Wells for, you won't get better than this. Not unless you tag along with the sheriff for another day or so.'

As Will's words took on meaning, everyone fell silent. Their nervous faces stared down at Painter as though a gun was going to appear from a fold of his long, grubby coat.

'I shot him in the execution of my duty,' Stone said. 'I was protecting the office.'

'Well you got the execution bit right. That's how you protect the office, and that's why the marshal's got to do something about it,' Will snapped back.

Chimes was in an uneasy, uncompromising situation. Gaining time, he closed his eyes and squeezed the bridge of his nose with the tips of his fingers. 'Hand over your gun, Sheriff,' he said after a moment. 'You don't give me much choice.'

'What the hell for? You're arresting me?' Stone demanded.

'Oh yeah, he's doing that,' Will answered. 'One of the advantages of having had time to read is you glean snippets of information that might come in handy one day. Like knowing there's a law against shooting someone in cold blood.'

Some called Rufus Stone 'Sheriff Stone Dead', or 'Rufus Heart of Stone'. But now the man looked in danger of breaking apart. Words of resentment and protest welled up in his mouth, then gave out. He could rant until daybreak if he wished, but nothing would change the facts. He avoided eye contact with the marshal as he handed him his gun, didn't look to Will or spare a glance at Eels Painter.

'The law's meant to work *for* you as well as *against*. So, we'll do our best to assist you,' Chimes declared. 'Must admit, it's not what I expected,' he added sombrely.

'It's not what any of us expected,' Oleg Halstom spoke up. 'But there's someone here who can't say the same. That's about right, isn't it, Will?' he said, his voice holding the shade of regret.

'What are you talking about?' Chimes demanded.

'I'm Oleg Halstrom. Editor of the *Basin Bugle*. And I'm saying that what we just saw here was an act of revenge, but not from Eels Painter, alone.' Halstrom's response was calm and measured. 'I can't prove it, but despite the feeling from Painter when he stood in that doorway, his words carried the intimidation of *him*,' he said, nodding towards Will Jarrow. 'He came to *our* town to bring our sheriff down and he's done it. That makes him as culpable as anyone else.'

Rufus Stone turned to Will, gave him a more penetrating look than ever before. 'Who the hell are you, mister?' he commanded.

'Halstrom just said,' Will replied evenly. 'I'm the man who's come to bring you down. And he's a newspaper man, so it must be the God's honest truth. But it's not just me, or Painter. There's been a hell of a lot of folk looking to your demise.'

'Who am I to you?' Stone barked in anger. 'What is it you're after?'

'I'll tell you who he is. You're going to find out sometime,' Halstrom interjected. 'He's the man your daughter hoped to marry.'

Stone stared, disbelief then understanding breaking across his hard features. 'You? You're the one?'

Will nodded. 'Yeah, I'm the one. And you're the one who robbed me and Natalie of a lifetime together. You couldn't abide her going against you, so you stopped her. You killed your own daughter with murderous, diehard arrogance.'

'Steady on, feller, that's inflammatory talk,' Chimes advised. 'I reckon we'd all best simmer down, while I hear the meat of this story.'

'Tell him, Will. Let's get it over with,' Halstrom said.

'Give you a goddamn story, you mean. That's about as far as your interest goes, Halstrom. Don't kid anyone it's about truthfulness.'

'It's through my columns that people will find out, goddamnit. Don't you want that?' Halstrom pressed.

'Those same people have been indulging their own killer for years. And from the safety of a lawman's badge,' Will countered. 'They don't need your newspaper to give them intimate details of a young girl's death. It would probably be no more than information to admire on Stone's office wall.'

Will turned his cold eyes back on Stone. 'As for you, there's no punishment to make up for what you did. But right now, I'd like to try and find one.'

At Will's caustic response, Stone roared an oath and snatched back his Colt from where Chimes had shoved it in his belt.

But Will was ready. It was a move he'd goaded the sheriff into, and he leaped forward, gripping the sheriff's wrist as men standing near scattered.

'God, I've taken out better than you,' Stone raged. 'It was you killed my little girl, you goddamn jailmeat.'

Will couldn't wrench the gun free, and a shot ripped into the ceiling. Even with one arm tied in a sling, Stone's strength was that of a crazy man. Will hauled his own Colt and rammed it hard and deep into Stone's belly.

'You're getting a long time to rue your life, Stone,' he said, almost breathing the words into the man's ear. 'I don't have to kill anybody, and old Painter got what he wanted, in the way he chose.'

Chimes looked on with seemingly detached interest. Halstrom and the horrified onlookers waited for the muffled report from Will's gun. In their eyes, his clash with Stone would now surely end as self-defence in his favour.

'The barrel of this Colt's so far into your gut no one will ever know you've been shot. They'll think it was the guilt you died of,' Will threatened. All he had to do was pull the trigger. But he couldn't. In settling the score on Rufus Stone, he'd gone as far as he was ever going to go.

'I'm not the killer I thought I could be,' he

muttered jadedly. 'Not like you.'

The frame of Stone's Colt crashed into Will's face with sickening force. Will gasped and staggered back a pace. In a moment, his victory had turned to ashes, and a vicious backhand made him drop his own Colt. Stone immediately chopped him in the neck, sending him to the puncheons. Stone was injured, having only one arm to fight effectively with. But the difference was that Will never had any stomach for killing, while the sheriff did, together with the reflexes for self-preservation.

Stone glared down at Will, took deliberate and steady aim between his eyes. 'You turned my daughter against me. You stole her. I've waited so long,' he added with rare emotion, putting first pressure on the trigger.

'It's been a long time for me too, Stone. Because of you, I've thought an' done things I never wanted to. So go ahead, pull the trigger. Live out the rest of your life with no one else to kill, you miserable son-of-a-bitch.'

A gun roared, but it wasn't Stone's. Stone just grunted, staring incredulously at the snub-nosed Colt that the Greenfield marshal had pulled from his shoulder holster. Then he gave a fleeting, defeated smile before his legs buckled him into a kneeling position. He took a last look at Will, shook his head tiredly and closed his eyes as he toppled sideways. But Warren Chimes was an expert shot, and Stone was dead before he hit the floor.

'I had to see it panning out. You got to be in little doubt before you kill someone,' Chimes said. ''Specially if it's a town sheriff.'

'You should have been here a couple of years ago to tell *him* that,' Will said thickly, gradually rising to his feet with help from Halstrom.

'It doesn't matter any more. I think Blue Wells has kicked off its hobble,' Halstrom said, and nobody thought or said different.

'You had the chance. Why didn't you pull the trigger?' Chimes asked.

'Who knows? Perhaps I had me all wrong,' Will replied.

'Either that or you'd learned something. You took the difficult path.'

'No offence, Marshal, but I really don't give a fig.'

'If that's true, you'd have shot him, and I'd be long gone.'

It was the following day and, as if acknowledging an opponent's defeat, the storm had veered east, leaving a trail of sodden devastation. The men were sitting in the jailhouse, and Will still didn't know if he was going to be charged. He'd not admitted complicity with Eels Painter and his arrival in town, but he suspected Marshal Chimes had put two and two together, especially after Oleg Halstrom's revelations.

Yet, Will genuinely didn't care. He'd spent two years living with hate, desperately wanting revenge on a man whose death now left him dejected and drained. *So why the hell do I care what anyone else has to say on the matter?* he thought to himself.

'You didn't shoot because you couldn't,' Chimes continued. 'And the reason you couldn't is because, once upon a time, you were a decent, law-abiding man. There's obviously been a few years when you more'n likely forgot, but now you can start again.'

'Thanks for the testament, Marshal. Does that mean I can ride on?'

'I guess so. You got somewhere in mind?'

'No, as long as it's a long, long way from here. Maybe I'll go and help 'em seek that north-west passage.'

'Huh. Why don't you stay?'

'Stay here? What the hell for?'

'This,' Chimes said, and tossed something onto

the desk.

Will grinned. 'You're joking,' he said, picking up Rufus Stone's badge of office.

'No. Just in case you hadn't noticed, I'm not one for acting the joker when I'm on duty. I *could* let you leave, even wish you bon voyage. But then we all lose. Fact is, this town needs someone who has a natural sense of justice, someone who doesn't pull triggers at the first sight of trouble. That's a valuable strength I've seen in you, Will Jarrow. It's certainly more of an opportunity than what you've been used to. At least *think* on it.'

'Yeah. Least I can do, when put like that,' Will responded. He knew it would take time to forget the recent past. But he wanted more than anything to clear his mind and get his life back. He would take a stroll along to Ma Kettle's Mercantile, see April Winney and take her to lunch. He could ask her what she thought of the offer, then return later in the day to pin on the sheriff's star, perhaps order up a new one.